# A DARING SACRIFICE

## Other books by Jody Hedlund

*An Uncertain Choice*
*The Vow: A novella*

# A DARING SACRIFICE

## JODY HEDLUND

ZONDERVAN

*A Daring Sacrifice*
Copyright © 2016 by Jody Hedlund

This title is also available as a Zondervan ebook. Visit www.zondervan.com/ebooks.

Requests for information should be addressed to:
Zondervan, 3900 *Sparks Dr. SE, Grand Rapids, Michigan* 49546

ISBN 978-0-310-74937-0

Cover design and photography: *Mike Heath / Magnus Creative*
Interior design: *Greg Johnson / Textbook Perfect*

Printed in the United States of America

16 17 18 19 20 21 22 23 /DCI/ 20 19 18 17 16 15 14 13 12 11 10 9 8 7 6 5 4 3 2 1

# Chapter 1

*Forests of Wessex*
*In the year of our Lord 1390*

*"Time to chop off your thumbs."* *The hulking soldier* pinched the back of my neck through the coarse wool of my cloak. The sharp pressure forced me to kneel in front of the flat stone. "Put out your hand, you poacher."

"You can't cut off my thumbs," I protested in a gruff voice I hoped disguised my true, girlish tone.

"For hunting on the Wessex land, I'm obliged to hack off the whole hand." The solider, who was as wide as an ox, shoved me so that my false, padded belly pushed into the rectangular slab. "Count yourself lucky that Sir Edgar is in a good mood today and only ordered the loss of your thumbs."

I glanced to the road, where Lord Wessex's son sat astride his fair steed. He was surrounded by several other noblemen and women. His deep laughter rose into the air, followed by a chorus of giggles from his female admirers.

The usual hot anger spurted in my blood. I knew they weren't laughing directly at me. Even so, I was incensed that they could find any reason for amusement at such a time. Had they no pity for an old man—what they thought me to be—who was about to be savagely maimed?

My gaze lingered on the fine silk gown of one of the young women, a deep purple hue strewn with intricately embroidered lace. She'd paired the dress with pure white gloves . . .and a pearl necklace. The pearls alone would buy enough grain to feed a dozen families for a week.

"Come now, old man. Don't make this any harder than need be." The soldier prodded my stooped shoulders. "Take the punishment you deserve." But even as he spoke, his gaze followed mine to Edgar, who took a swig from a flask and then passed it to a friend. When I glanced back to the soldier, his lips were pursed at the sight of Edgar's revelry.

"No one deserves this." I bent my head and made my voice raspy. I wore my long hair tucked under a man's linen coif and had smeared mud over my face, but if Sir Edgar or the soldiers took a closer look at me, they'd surely see past the disguise. They'd discover the *cloaked bandit* they were looking for. And I'd potentially lose much more than my thumbs.

The tall soldier on the other side of the stone yawned and then unsheathed his hunting knife. The long silver blade glinted in the autumn afternoon sunlight.

"Lord Wessex won't miss a couple of squirrels," I spoke quickly. Time was running out. I had to figure out a way to make my escape. "Especially squirrels as scrawny as those." I nodded at the stiff creatures lying only feet away, next to my bow and quiver.

Even though I wasn't truly afraid yet, I could feel a sense of urgency beginning to take hold. My fingers twitched with the need to reach for my weapon. But with the ox at my back and tall guard across from me, I would have to make my move at just the right time. Besides, there were at least two other soldiers on the perimeter that I would be forced to outmaneuver.

I eyed the brambles and dark shadows of the surrounding forest. If I released my arrows while sprinting, I might be able to eliminate two of the guards and reach the cover of trees before the others could react.

"Doesn't matter what you take from Lord Wessex's land." The bulky girth of the soldier behind me pressed into my body, pinning me against the stone. "Stealing is stealing."

I resisted his hold. "How can it be stealing when Lord Wessex doesn't give us any place to hunt and no means to keep our families from dying of hunger?"

The soldier faltered.

"Please," I whispered. "Have mercy. My boy is all I have left. And he's always hungry. I'm sure you have a growing son and know how much food such children need to survive." Although I had no son, I prayed my words would earn the soldier's sympathy.

The ox heaved a breath laden with garlic and onion, and his grip slackened.

Maybe more of the populace was dissatisfied with Lord Wessex's leadership than I realized. My father had always believed the people should rise up and fight against the oppression—that in their hearts they disliked Lord Wessex's tactics, and that with the right leadership they could over-throw him.

Had my father been right?

I gave myself a mental shake. His faith in the populace had been his downfall. And I wouldn't repeat his mistake.

"What's taking so long?" came Sir Edgar's irritated call from the road. "Must I come over and do the deed myself?"

I had the urge to stand, face Edgar, and dare him to try. I'd been waiting for years to spit into his face. If he came anywhere near me, I probably wouldn't be able to resist the urge, even if it would lead to my death.

The tall soldier concealed another yawn and shook his head. "No, sir. We're ready." He lifted his knife.

But the hefty soldier behind me didn't move. No doubt he was thinking that if I lost my thumbs, I would be maimed for life. Most of the men who lost their fingers or thumbs were rendered useless as hunters, and many of them could no longer ply their trades. Their already starving families suffered even more.

"Cut off his thumbs now," Edgar shouted. "Or I shall cut off your hands."

The ox released another garlicky sigh and then forced my arm upward onto the stone.

I was strong for a girl of seventeen. But I couldn't resist the muscle of a full-grown soldier, let alone one who was at least double the width of a normal man. He pushed my gloved hand down against the smooth stone. The rusty stains on the rock reminded me that too many men had lost a limb upon this ledge.

The heat of anger seeped deeper into my soul. If only I could do more to alleviate the suffering of the peasants . . .

As it was, I tirelessly labored day after day to provide for the many families who'd been driven from their homes and from honest work. And as time passed, more and more came to depend upon me for food and shelter . . . because of Lord Wessex's greed and cruelty.

"Spread your fingers." The soldier behind me pushed my palm flat. With brute strength, he plied my fingers wider, and then nodded at his tall companion wielding the knife.

I tensed. What if my plan of escape didn't work? What if the ox didn't loosen his hold on my wrist? What if I sprang a moment too late? Beneath the layers of my disguise, a trickle of sweat made an itchy line between my shoulder blades. Even though the hint of cooler weather was in the air, the sunshine of the fall day was still warm.

The soldier began to lower the knife, and I readied myself to dodge the blow.

"Wait," the ox bellowed, making me jump. "We need to take off his gloves first."

"No," I replied.

His offer was likely made out of compassion. The gloves would impede the blade and make the severing more time-consuming. Having one's thumb hacked off in slow increments would be infinitely more painful than a swift, clean chop.

While I appreciated his kindness, I couldn't risk taking off my gloves. I might be able to hide my features in the mud and the shadows of my hat. And I could pad my tunic and trousers to make myself look like a frumpy, stoop-shouldered old man. But if I took off my gloves, they would see my fingers. Even though they were cracked and creased with dirt, there would be no hiding the fact that they were long, slender, and womanly. I would give away my cover, and in the process chance losing my slight window to break free.

The soldier holding the knife drew back.

"What now?" Edgar shouted.

"Hurry and take off his gloves." The tall soldier waved the blade impatiently.

"Just cut through them," I said, and this time I splayed my hands willingly.

The soft *jay-jay* of a blue jay called from the treetops, which had already begun to change into their vibrant arrays of gold and crimson. I tried to pretend I hadn't heard anything.

"'Twill be easier on you to have a clean cut," the soldier behind me insisted.

'Twould most definitely not go easier on me. Not when they realized my true gender. Not when they then unmasked me further and realized I was the bandit who was terrorizing Wessex lands.

And it would go even worse if Sir Edgar and his father saw my red hair and my cleaned face and eventually figured out the vigilante they had sought was the rightful heir to Wessex, that I hadn't died alongside my father after all.

"Let's have the gloves, old man." The ox began wrestling my hand and tugging at the leather hugging my fingertips.

"No!" I shouted, this time forgetting to disguise my voice.

At the sound of my much higher, clearer tone, the bulky soldier loosened his grasp. The fraction was all I needed. I yanked away, dropped to the ground, and rolled toward my bow. In an instant I had it in hand with an arrow notched and drawn.

I jumped up and was on my feet, running while shooting the arrow in the direction of one of the perimeter guards. It hit him squarely in his fighting hand, as I'd intended. The arrow had hardly left my bow before I had another pulled back and ready to loose.

But another arrow flew out of the forest nearby and hit the second perimeter guard before I could let go. I didn't stop running to think. I simply shot my arrow at the tall soldier with the knife, making sure it knocked the weapon from his raised hand rather than piercing him.

I sprinted toward the forest edge and glanced again at the noblewoman and the pearls. Did I have time to get what I'd been after in the first place?

Two horses with their riders burst through the forest and stampeded across the clearing. Amidst the shouting and chaos, I relished the sound of Sir Edgar's curses. Did Edgar really think he'd get to entertain his guests at my expense today? If so, then my cousin was stupider than he looked.

One of the horses pounded closer, and when a hand reached down for me, I latched on and swung myself up behind the young rider.

I put my head down and kicked my heels into the flank of the beast, urging it faster.

An arrow zipped past us.

I spun as much as I could on the bare back of the horse. One of Sir Edgar's friends and fellow noblemen had shot at me. I took aim and released my arrow with a ping. It ripped across the distance, and within seconds sliced through the man's hat, knocking it from his head, parting his hair and skimming his scalp in the process.

I watched him long enough to see shock widen his eyes. Then I turned back and grinned.

The horse plunged into the brambles and the darkness of the woods. I grabbed onto the rider to keep from toppling off. We charged through the tangle of trees and brush, the branches whipping us, thorns grabbing our tunics, and the windfall threatening to trip us.

But the horse didn't slacken its pace. Nor did the steed behind us.

A quick glance over my shoulder revealed Bulldog. His fleshy face was dark with anger and his scowl chastised me. His blue jay call had alerted me to his presence, and I was glad for his help. But I could have made my escape without him—I usually managed. There had been no need for him to put his and Thatch's lives in danger on account of me.

I crouched low behind Thatch, Bulldog's son. Thatch's blond hair stuck up on his head like dry straw. I gripped him tightly, and his boney body felt as thin as twigs beneath the thin, tattered clothes he wore. Together we swayed with the horse's movements, ducking low and making the kind of getaway we'd accomplished plenty of times over the past few years.

We rode hard for many long minutes, putting the distance we needed between ourselves and Sir Edgar. Thatch wisely guided the horses far from our forest home. We would likely have to spend the next day or two eluding soldiers before we could make our way back to the secret caverns, which served as the base of operations as well as shelter for the many people we helped.

When we finally reached a narrow gully, we reined our horses and hid in the shadows for several moments, our heavy breathing mingling with the snorting of the horses.

Bulldog grabbed my sleeve and growled, "Young missy, I ought to take a switch to your backside for that stunt."

"That wasn't a stunt. I was fishing. For pearls." Technically, I'd been hunting. But I hadn't been able to resist trailing the noblewoman once I'd spotted the necklace.

"It was the stupidest thing you've done to date, and that's saying something, because you've done plenty of foolish things."

"We're running low on provisions."

Bulldog folded his thick arms across his chest as if restraining himself from strangling me. "I know we'll need to make a raid soon. But not on Sir Edgar. And definitely not when you're by yourself."

"I had everything under control the whole time." Or at least mostly. "I could have gotten away just fine."

His dark eyebrows came together into a thunderous glare above his equally black eyes. "Or you could have ended up like this." He held up his hands. I didn't have to look to know what he was referring to. But my gaze was nevertheless drawn to the stumps where his thumbs had once been.

Bulldog was one of the lucky ones who'd only lost his thumbs for poaching. And he was also one of the most stubborn, determined, and strong men I'd ever met. It was due to those qualities alone he'd learned to shoot his bow again, unlike so many men who were crippled for life.

Thatch peered up at me with adoring eyes. "I think all Dad is trying to say is that, next time, make sure you bring me along. That way I can help you."

I smiled at the boy and tousled his hair, which only made the strands stand up farther.

He gave me one of his wide, crooked smiles, which revealed the gap in the top where he'd lost one of his front teeth in a fist fight.

Bulldog snarled. "That's not what I'm saying at all."

Thatch's grin slipped away.

"I trust Thatch to watch out for you," Bulldog said, softening at the sight of disappointment in his son's face. "But, Juliana, I gave your father my word that I'd protect you with my life. How can I do that if you're constantly charging into dangerous situations without telling me?"

The braying of a hound wafted on the wind.

Bulldog didn't have to say anything. One grimace of his rounded face was all it took to know his frustration. Sir Edgar already had men tracking us.

Thatch sprang onto the back of his mare and offered me his hand. I swung up behind him at the same time that Bulldog mounted his horse. He lifted his short nose and sniffed the air. Then he cocked his ear and listened intently.

"We'll have to split up," he said in a voice tight with frustration. "I'll lead them on a wild goose chase. And the two of you get as far away from here as you can."

For a moment, remorse tumbled about my empty stomach. Danger was nothing new. We'd lived with threats, starvation, and menace every day in the three years since my father had attempted his revolt and subsequently lost his life. But I didn't like the thought that I'd made things harder for Bulldog and Thatch with my recklessness. "I'm sorry—"

"I'm tired of your apologies." Bulldog's keen eyes swept through the dense forest. The thick tamarack and low spruce would slow down the search party, but the hunting dogs would eventually sniff out our trails.

"I'll go on by myself." I wiped a sleeve across my mud-caked face, brushing away sweaty flecks of dirt.

"No," Bulldog replied tersely. "Thatch will stay with you."

I held back my protest. I'd already rankled Bulldog enough for one day. Even though I didn't need Thatch's help, I liked his company. If Bulldog was forcing me to flee, at least I wouldn't be bored with Thatch along.

The barking of the dogs sounded nearer.

"Head west of Wessex. And stay out of the forest for three days." Bulldog bolted out of the gully, his steed crunching through the fallen leaves.

Thatch tugged his horse toward the west but paused when Bulldog glanced at us over his broad shoulder.

"Be careful." Bulldog's voice was harsh, but his eyes gentled as his gaze touched first on Thatch and then me.

"We'll be fine," I reassured him.

He gave a curt nod, then kicked his horse forward and was gone.

Thatch murmured to his mare and spurred her into the dense foliage.

I'd much rather be the one racing through the forest, dodging Lord Wessex's soldiers. There was something wild and exciting about the chase. But I'd accept the wisdom of Bulldog's plans this time. Maybe I had stepped too far over the line of danger with my latest move.

At the very least, it wouldn't hurt to lay low for a few days—especially for everyone else's sakes. The last thing I wanted to do was endanger Bulldog, Thatch, and the other families.

The wind and branches whipped my face.

Bulldog had told us to head west. West of Wessex. My mind spun with the possibilities . . .fishing possibilities.

I'd heard rumors that the master of the land bordering Wessex on the west had finally returned after years of being gone. The young, wealthy master who'd once insulted my red hair. An insult I'd never forgotten or forgiven.

A smile tugged at my lips.

"Head to Goodrich land," I called to Thatch.

Yes, indeed. I sensed some very good fishing possibilities ahead.

# Chapter 2

I GAVE MY STEED FULL REIN, LETTING MY MOUNT PLOD AT a leisurely pace. The morning air was crisp, finally losing the heat of the summer. A breeze ruffled my cloak and tugged at my cap.

Irene and our two guests rode ahead with the servants and huntsmen, and for a reason I couldn't understand I was content to lag behind. I hadn't even brought my falcon as the others had. In fact, I'd almost decided to stay at the manor. After the past four weeks of partying and dancing and feasting, I expected to be much happier than I found myself now.

Of course I was glad to be home, to see my sister, and to reacquaint myself with friends of the family. I'd only returned home twice in the many years I'd served as a squire and then as a knight under the Noblest Knight—once when my stepmother had died, and then three years ago, after my father had passed on.

Now that Father was gone, as the only son I'd inherited everything—the lands, estates, and fortune. I was quite likely the wealthiest man in all the kingdom, next to the High King.

I had everything I wanted. I should feel satisfied . . .But with each passing day, I only grew more restless.

Ahead, Irene smiled at the man riding next to her. Her falcon perched on her wrist, grasping the long leather glove she wore. The tiny bell on the falcon's foot tinkled just like her laughter.

As Irene was now nineteen and past due for marriage, my first task was to find my sister a good husband. As lord of Goodrich, it was my duty now. So even though I'd considered canceling the festivities she'd arranged for my homecoming, I'd continued with her plans for her sake.

If I couldn't cheer myself through the endless merriment, perhaps at the very least I would be able to find her a perfect match. Once she was safely married, then maybe I'd return to the Noblest Knight, the Duke of Rivenshire. Serving alongside my mentor had been much more exciting than my current situation.

I glanced through the canopy of changing leaves to the blue sky overhead. Perhaps if I just tried harder to be content with my new life . . .

A sudden glint in the branches of a nearby maple tree caught my eye—the glint of a knife.

I stiffened but forced myself to remain casual even as my mind raced forward.

We were about to be ambushed.

I began to whistle a merry tune. As lazily as I could, I stretched my arms above my head and used the movement to assess the surroundings better. From what I could tell, there was only one bandit in the tree.

As I lowered my hand, I brushed the goose feather fletching on one arrow in my belt quiver. If I wanted, I could shoot the thief out of the tree before he knew what hit him.

But as the man shifted into a crouch on the branch that hung above our path, I let my hand fall to my side. From the litheness and lightness of the figure, I guessed the bandit was nothing more than a child. I wouldn't—couldn't—hurt a child. But I also wouldn't sit by if the wayward urchin jumped onto my sister and attempted to harm her in any way.

My fingers slid to the knife sheathed underneath my tunic.

Completely unaware of the danger above us, Irene and our guests passed under the branch. My muscles tensed in readiness, but I continued to whistle as if I hadn't a care in the world.

When I neared the tree, I tried to keep myself from glancing up. From the corner of my eye, I could see the waif and his outstretched knife. As I finally passed beneath the danger, for a second I could almost believe that we'd avoided an altercation, that perhaps the young boy was simply hiding and feared detection.

But at a whoop from the branches and a crash behind me, I knew my wishes were in vain. The pressure at my backside was quickly followed by the sharpness of a blade against my neck.

Irene screamed. The guests shouted. And the horses stamped nervously, whinnying as they halted ahead of me.

"Don't move," came the voice of the urchin. "None of you move! Or I'll slit his throat."

At the threat, the boy brought the knife around into clearer view.

Irene's already pale face turned almost translucent. The two men riding next to her froze. One of the huntsmen farther ahead had already drawn his sword, but at the sight of the knife angled against my throat, he slowly lowered his weapon.

My fingers slid toward my knife.

But the child was smarter than I anticipated. Before I could stop him, he unsheathed my blade and tossed it into the forest. Another young boy charged out of the brush, this one on a horse. He caught my knife and held it in one hand, aimed and ready to throw at the noblemen or servants if they moved.

"What do you want?" I asked, assessing how I could take down both of the boys if they became too threatening.

The boy behind me shifted. "Nice of you to ask, Master Collin—or should I now say Sir Collin?"

"Lord Collin," I stated with as much nonchalance as I could muster. I could easily snap the boy's wrist and put an arrow into his accomplice before either of them could react. But I made myself wait patiently. "Do I know you, son?"

The boy gave a low chuckle. "It's been a while, *Lord* Collin." The emphasis on my title was mocking.

I tried to place the voice, but from the strain in the child's tone I could tell that he was working to disguise himself from recognition. Who was this? Suddenly I was more curious than nervous. I wanted to spin around and take stock of the boy. But I also knew I couldn't underestimate the two youths.

Instead I glanced at the boy on the horse. His blond hair stuck up on end, his face was thin and freckled, and he was slight of frame. If I had to guess his age, I'd estimate twelve years and no more. The boy behind me sounded slightly older.

"So how can I help you today?" I asked casually, as if I made an everyday practice of bargaining with young bandits.

"You can help by giving us this." With a flick of the knife, the young man behind me loosened the gold chain holding my cloak closed. He flicked the chain toward his friend, who caught it one-handed without so much as blinking.

My cloak fell away, revealing my jewel-studded mantle.

"And you can most certainly help by giving us this." The tip of the knife slashed into the linen of the mantle, cutting it away.

Inwardly, I flinched, waiting for the knife to pierce my shoulder. But to my surprise, the boy divested me of the garment and flung it toward his friend without so much as nicking my flesh.

Then before I could react, the boy stood on my horse, and with perfect balance leaped off and landed behind his accomplice. Their mare seemed prepared for the jarring movement of receiving the new rider, obviously having been through the routine plenty of other times.

Several of the huntsmen raised their weapons and began to move toward the bandits, but I held up my hand to stop them. Surely my servants had heard of my daring deeds in battle, and knew I could disarm these two waifs by myself if I chose to do so.

As the thief clutched his accomplice, I could see the size difference. The thief was just as thin as the boy, but taller and definitely older.

Their horse shied back. Only then did I get a glimpse of the thief's face beneath the hood of a cloak. Though remnants of dried mud peeled away from his nose and forehead, I could see past the thin disguise to elegant cheekbones, a gracefully curved chin, and full lips. Such features couldn't belong to a boy.

No. This was no boy.

This was a woman.

I had to rapidly conceal my surprise by side-stepping away from the bandits. I didn't want her to know I'd discovered the truth about her disguise. Not yet.

"Is there anything more you'd like to steal from me today?" I asked while twisting at the jewel on my finger. "Perhaps my ring?"

A flicker of surprise lit her eyes—dark brown irises that were framed by long, thick lashes.

I tossed the ring at her. She caught it with ease.

I could see that she was working to keep her face blank, to conceal her surprise. But she wasn't nearly as well trained as I was in such tactics.

I smothered a grin.

She tucked the ring into the bag at her accomplice's side. "You're too kind, Lord Collin." Again her tone had a hint of sarcasm.

"You're welcome."

"I didn't thank you."

"That's not very nice of you." I couldn't stop my grin any more than I could stop the words.

"I was nice enough not to slice your throat open."

I laughed then. I couldn't help myself.

Didn't she know I could have easily overtaken her and her partner if I'd wanted to? I could have killed them both in a matter of seconds. I'd trained with the Duke of Rivenshire for years next to the toughest knights in all the land. I'd fought in more battles than I could count. I was likely the best bowman in the entire kingdom.

Her eyes narrowed and her fingers crept toward the half-empty quiver at her side.

With a nod and another grin, I spun my horse away from her. I could tell she wanted to shoot me but that she wouldn't. There was something too kind about her eyes, too level-headed. She might be a thief, but she was no murderer.

I urged my mount toward Irene and our guests but couldn't resist a parting shot over my shoulder. "If you ever need anything more, don't hesitate to stop me again."

Her eyes flashed. And for a moment I had the feeling I'd looked into those brown eyes before, that I'd experienced the churning anger in them once upon a time.

But before I could question her, she pulled her hood forward and gave a low command. The urchin in front of her bent low and kicked their horse into motion. Within seconds they'd disappeared completely, swallowed by the thick forest. The huntsmen began to spur their horses and dogs into a chase, but I sidled in front of them, blocking their path.

"Let them go," I called, staring at the spot where they'd disappeared. My heart hammered with the need to follow them, to find out who she was. But Irene had already moved to my side, having given the care of her falcon to one of the servants.

"My lord." Her voice quivered. "Are you hurt?"

"Not in the least." I studied the bend of the branches, the crush of the dried leaves, and the slight imprint of the horse's hooves.

Irene pressed a lacey handkerchief to her eyes and dabbed away moisture. "I have been dreading the day when something like this might happen here on our land."

The young noblemen nodded and offered platitudes to comfort her. For a moment, I couldn't even remember their names. All I could think about were my friends, Sir Derrick and Sir Bennet, and how if they'd been there, they would have been by my side, lending me their unconditional support and companionship. The despondency from earlier sifted over me again.

"So far, the thievery has only happened on neighboring lands," Irene was saying. "But now it appears we are to suffer the same fate."

"Perhaps the Cloaked Bandit is behind this," said one of the noblemen.

"Cloaked Bandit?" I asked, my mind already tracking the young woman through the woods. I could find her if I wanted. She'd left a careless trail.

"Lord Wessex has been trying to capture a thief everyone calls the Cloaked Bandit," Irene started.

I snorted, expecting Irene to smile and tell me she was only jesting.

But Irene's pale face remained serious. Her lips pursed together in displeasure at my humor. She sat tall and straight on her mare, her blond hair and green eyes so much like my own. But our similarities ended with appearances, at least as far as I could tell.

I hadn't really known my sister while growing up, since I'd lived with the Duke of Rivenshire during my training toward knighthood. But while reacquainting myself with her over the past month, I'd realized we were as different as summer and winter.

And she reminded me too much of our father.

"I beg your pardon, sister," I offered with as much sincerity as I could muster. "I didn't realize you were serious about this—this Cloaked Bandit."

"Of course I am." She lifted her chin. "The thief has been giving Lord Wessex trouble for the past year, so much so that now there's a bounty on his head."

I had met George Wessex and his son at one of Irene's feasts. There I had learned that while I'd been gone serving in campaigns with the duke, George had marched in and taken the estate away from his half brother, Charles, claiming their father had left it to him. Apparently none of the other lords from the surrounding lands—including my father—defended Charles for fear of repercussions from George's strong band of loyal knights and warriors. George had banished his brother without challenge and taken control of Wessex. Charles eventually perished, although I was still unclear how. I hadn't exactly been impressed with the new heir to Wessex, or his son. But it had been obvious that they admired Irene.

"And what is this cloaked bandit's crime?"

"Why stealing, of course," Irene answered.

"Surely, it must be more serious than that if Lord Wessex put a bounty on the man's head."

"He evades capture," one of the noblemen chimed in.

"That's no fault of the Cloaked Bandit." I again glanced at the forest and the gentle shadows of the shifting trees. "If Lord Wessex were competent—"

"The Cloaked Bandit has amassed a group of followers," Irene continued. "And they live in the forests of Wessex."

Surprise once again nudged me. "What's wrong with Lord Wessex that so many people dislike him?"

"I've heard complaints of his high taxes," Irene admitted. "But that's no excuse for stealing. Sin is sin. And we cannot turn a blind eye to crime, or the other peasants will think such behavior is acceptable."

"Has Lord Wessex considered lowering his taxes?"

Irene smiled stiffly, almost patronizing me. "Brother, you've never had an inclination for business affairs. And besides, after being gone these many years, how can you know what it takes to manage a vast estate?"

I nodded. I didn't have one ounce of concern about the management of our wealth. I never had. In fact, as long as I could do as I pleased with my money, I didn't care what William, my steward, did with the estate, or how he did it. I trusted our old servant to take care of things as he always had.

"We need to inform the sheriff," Irene said, spurring her horse around the way we'd already come. "We need to find these thieves and punish them."

The noblemen followed her.

I stared at the forest for a moment longer, wishing I could leave the hunting party posthaste and follow the young pair of thieves. I'd have an easier time by the light of day. But the cover of darkness would give me an element of surprise. I didn't want the bandits bolting before I could discover all I needed about them.

"In fact, I think I shall induce our sheriff to form a search party," Irene called.

"There's no need," I said, trotting after her.

"Of course there is," she countered. "We don't want our people thinking thievery is acceptable on our lands. We must punish it severely and swiftly and set an example of intolerance, or we may end up with the same out-of-control problems Lord Wessex has."

"No. We shall let the boys go," I said more firmly. I was, after all, the lord now. My sister may have been in charge since our father died. But she didn't need to be any longer.

She cast me a sideways glance, opened her mouth to speak, but then clamped her lips shut.

"If they had need to steal my trinkets," I said, "then they must have greater want of them than I do."

"Trinkets?"

"I have plenty more rings and chains and mantles." We had riches beyond measure. More than any one man needed.

Irene didn't respond for a moment, and when she did her voice was tight and low. "Our father worked incredibly hard over the years to elevate our family's position and fortune. You can't come home and throw it all away."

I sensed a threat to her words. But I didn't care. "Let them go, Irene," I responded. "It's my wealth now. And I can do with it what I want."

Irene bowed her head in compliance, as a younger sister should. But something about the tight lines in her face told me she didn't like my order. Not in the least.

# Chapter 3

*"Dad will boil you alive when he finds out about* your stunt," Thatch whispered through chattering teeth.

In the darkness of the forest, with just the sliver of moon overhead, Thatch was mostly invisible. But I could feel his thin body shivering next to mine.

"Bulldog will be happy enough once I show him our loot," I whispered back, pushing down the guilt that kept trying to surface.

I did indeed have remorse after evaluating what I'd done in my raid against Collin Goodrich. But only a twinge, and only because of the effect my rashness was having upon Thatch.

As a precaution, I hadn't dared start a fire. I didn't yet know if the new Lord Goodrich would send out a search party for us. I was waiting for the deep hours of the night, when the possibility of detection was slim.

Now Thatch was shuddering in the rapidly dropping temperatures of the fall night. The gurgle of his belly rose in the silent air, reminding me that we hadn't eaten all day either.

The guilt prodded me harder. We could have hidden on Goodrich land in relative ease—if I'd laid low, which was exactly what Bulldog had ordered me to do. And Thatch was right. His dad was going to scold me upside and down for putting us in more danger.

But I hadn't been able to stop myself, especially when I'd caught sight of Collin Goodrich lagging behind the rest of his hunting party.

The opportunity had been too perfect, too easy, too fun to pass up.

Thatch shuddered again, his boney shoulder poking against my arm.

I shifted against the gnarled oak and tugged off my cloak. "Here. Cover yourself with this." I tossed the cloak over him.

"No!" His voice was laced with horror, and he shoved the garment away. "I'm not a weakling."

"You're freezing. And it's my fault."

"I'm not that cold." But even as he spoke, the words wobbled between his clattering teeth.

I pushed the heavy woolen garment back over him. "Don't make me tie you up."

"You wouldn't."

"Try me."

His thin body stiffened. And I could picture the waves of emotions rippling across his freckled face as he debated whether I was serious enough to follow through with my threat.

I smiled, glad for the darkness that hid my humor.

"Fine," he finally said, breathing out a heavy sigh. He knew me well enough to realize I didn't make idle threats. He squirmed for a moment as he adjusted my cloak over his limbs.

A breeze snaked through the thick branches overhead and rattled the dry leaves. It slithered around me and wound its way under my tunic, sending goose bumps up my back. I crossed my arms over my chest to ward off the cold. If anyone had to suffer for our current situation, I should be the one. Thatch certainly wasn't at fault.

In fact, he shouldn't have to suffer at all.

Deep anguish and anger rolled together in my chest, as it did whenever I thought of the unfairness of life for Thatch and the many others who'd been displaced from their homes because of Lord Wessex's high taxes and unfair laws.

My fingers groped for the coarse grain sack at my side, sliding over the lumps made by the few items inside. I found the small circular bump that I'd gone back to again and again.

Collin Goodrich's ring. He'd given me his ring. *Given* it to me.

I couldn't stop from picturing him as I had a hundred times since I'd robbed him that morning. Beneath his cap, his tousled hair had hung in unruly waves over his forehead, and it was the same blond he'd had as a young boy when I'd last seen him. His eyes were the same bright green that had stared at me when I'd been a small girl riding at my father's side.

But he wasn't a boy anymore. Not by any measure.

His features were but a shadow of the boy he'd once been; still as arrogantly handsome but in a much stronger, surer, and dashing way. He'd looked imposing atop his steed, his muscles rippling in his arms and beneath the tight linen of his breeches. I'd almost hesitated in my plans to jump on his horse.

But when he'd released a carefree whistle, I hadn't been able to resist. The liveliness of his tune, the jaunt of his head, and the leisureliness of his personhood had reminded me why I was living in the forest like a hunted animal.

It was because of rich noblemen like him that families were hiding, living in dirt hovels, and scrounging to find food to eat.

He'd deserved my attack. He wouldn't miss a single item I'd taken. And in the big cities and seaports, Bulldog would find his contacts, those who would gladly accept the jewels in exchange for necessities—such as heavier clothing and blankets for my friends, hopefully enough to keep them warm through the looming days of winter.

I'd done nothing for which I needed to be ashamed.

Why then did my fingers keep straying to his ring? And why did that long-forgotten ghost of my conscience rise to taunt me? Why were there whispers urging me to find a better way to provide for all of the people who depended upon me?

I thought I'd buried my conscience the same day I'd buried the chopped remains of my father's tortured body, gathered after he'd been drawn and quartered.

The *whoo-whoo* of an owl echoed in the crisp night air, but besides that and Thatch's chattering, the night remained silent. My gaze swept the dark outlines around me, assessing the woods for any danger as I still tried to shake the feeling I'd done something wrong.

Yes, stealing was wrong. I knew that. But what other choice did we have? I'd discussed the options with Bulldog countless times. And the truth of the matter was that if we hoped to keep everyone alive, we had to break the law.

We were only taking back from Lord Wessex the excess he'd taken from us, we'd told ourselves. We wouldn't need to steal from him if he hadn't stolen from us first.

My fingers traced the outline of Collin's ring.

So why had I stolen from Collin? He hadn't taken anything from me.

"O Father in heaven," I whispered, and buried my face into my hands. What was happening to me? Was I losing my sense of right and wrong completely? Was justifying my sins only leading me to slip further and further down a path toward more depravity?

Maybe I'd eventually end up being no better than Lord Wessex.

Was that what my father had feared? Was that why he'd remained so noble until the day he'd died?

Next to me, Thatch put a steadying hand upon my arm. "We'll be all right."

I reached into the sack and let my fingers linger over the cold silver band. I traced the engraved lines that wrapped around a cross made from embedded diamonds. Then I slipped the ring over one of my slender fingers.

It was much too big and only made me think about Collin's hands, how thick and strong his fingers probably were. I shifted the ring to my thumb and wedged it there.

Should I return his belongings? Maybe at first light I could sneak close to the gatehouse of his castle and toss the bag to one of his guards.

And yet . . . I leaned my head back and stared through the branches overhead, branches that would soon be bare and covered with frost. Something within me stubbornly resisted the idea of humbling myself before him. I set my lips together in a firm line and pushed all thoughts of remorse away.

He'd laughed at me. Again.

Thinking of his laughter both now and in the past only made me lift my chin.

Of course, his laughter back when I'd been just a girl of five had caused me to react childishly, earning me a rare rebuke from my father. When my father and I had finally ridden away and I'd glanced back at Collin through my hot tears, he'd been wearing that same wide grin he'd flashed at me today. It had been the last time I'd seen Collin. I'd later heard he'd gone to live with the Duke of Rivenshire.

At least I'd handled myself better now. I'd controlled my anger, even though I'd been sorely tempted to shoot the smile from his face.

"What kind of man willingly gives thieves his jewels?" I muttered.

"A very wealthy man?" Thatch asked, pulling my cloak halfway over my arm and scooting closer to me.

"And what kind of man gives permission to rob him again?"

"A *very*, very wealthy man?"

"He's cocky and prideful and thinks he's God's gift to the world."

At the barest crack of a branch behind us, I stiffened and fell silent. I dislodged Collin's ring and stuffed it into my pocket. Then my fingers slid to the knife that was sheathed at my waist. But instead of landing upon the carved handle, my fingers grasped at the air.

"My knife," I whispered, slapping the ground and patting at the leaves and twigs. "Where did it go?"

Had it fallen out? But even as I entertained the thought, I cast it aside. My weapon was too embedded into its sheath to slip out without my being aware.

"Did you take my knife?" I started to rise, but before I could react a gloved hand circled around my face and closed over my mouth, cutting off my words and any chance I had at screaming.

"Yes, I did take your knife," came a low voice near my ear.

I jerked against the hand, trying to free myself, but the grip was immovable. My captor was already hoisting me away from Thatch,

"I don't have my knife either," Thatch called out. I could hear him fumbling in the dry leaves, crawling around in a frantic search. "And my bow and arrows are gone too."

I kicked my captor's shins and tried to pummel him with my fists. But he clamped first one arm and then the other behind my back, effortlessly pinning them both. My mind shouted at me to do something—anything—to free myself.

In all the time I'd been hunted as the Cloaked Bandit, I'd never failed to get away from anyone. Sure, I'd been caught— like I had yesterday—but somehow I'd always managed to find a way to free myself. Or Bulldog had come to my rescue.

Even with my desperate kicking and jerking, my captor hauled me farther from Thatch, managing to slip through the thick brush as though a trail were emblazoned there.

Thatch's worried voice grew fainter. I prayed that in the blackness of the night, without his weapons, the boy wouldn't attempt to search for me, that he would stay with the horse and wait for the first light of morning to begin tracking me.

Unless I could free myself first.

I tried swinging my head to get a glimpse of my kidnapper, but the hand over my mouth made my head immovable.

Whoever had captured me was obviously a strong man. And my efforts to overpower him were doing little good, except to wear myself out.

Maybe I needed to try another tactic. If I cooperated, I could possibly get him to relax his hold. Then, at just the right moment, I might be able to break free and disappear into the woods.

I stopped struggling and let my body grow limp, even though every muscle urged me to keep fighting. After all, I was alone in a dark forest with a strange man. There was no telling who he was working for and where he was taking me. With a bounty on my head, there were any number of men who might be searching for me, hoping to bring me to Lord Wessex and earn a purse of silver.

But even with the slackening of my body, and even with my lack of resistance, my captor's hold over my mouth and arms didn't waver. He continued to force me to move backward, slowly but steadily.

Suddenly, all I could think was that this was it. He would lock me up in a dungeon somewhere and Thatch wouldn't be able to find me. Or even if my friend managed to track me, he'd be incapable of getting me out. And this time, Bulldog wouldn't be able to charge to my rescue. I'd have to rely upon my own ingenuity to escape.

Eventually, I would. I had no doubt about that. Even so, for the first time since my father died, I felt utterly alone. And I didn't like the feeling one bit.

# Chapter
## 4

EVEN THOUGH I HADN'T WANDERED THE FORESTS IN YEARS, the layout and the trail paths came back to me, making me feel as if I were still that boy of seven who had roamed the woodlands, instead of a man of twenty.

Not even the darkness of the night had impeded my search. Of course I'd gone out earlier in the evening, while I still had light. And I'd easily discovered all I needed to know.

"Too bad you were so sloppy and didn't cover your tracks," I said against the ear of my captive.

She'd finally stopped struggling, and I guessed she'd only done so to throw me off guard, to get me to release my grasp so that she could attempt an escape.

But I wasn't planning to discharge her until I discovered who she was and what she was doing on my land. She was obviously a fighter, but she'd learn soon enough that she was no match for me.

My backside bumped into the flank of my steed once I reached the narrow gorge where I'd left the beast. "I'm going to uncover your mouth," I said. "But if you scream or make any loud noises, I'll have to take drastic measures to make sure you're quiet."

She gave an almost imperceptible nod.

Slowly, I loosened my grasp over her mouth. When I lifted my hand away completely, I let it hover for a moment, waiting to see if she'd cooperate.

She remained silent, likely realizing that screaming wouldn't do her any good, especially since her companion was weaponless and would have a difficult time following us in the dark.

Without relaxing my hold on her arms, I twisted her around until she faced me. Before she could struggle, I quickly and easily used one hand to pin her thin wrists in front of her.

A shaft of moonlight broke through a gap in the gnarled branches overhead. The glow illuminated her face, showing her to indeed be the young thief who had attacked me earlier in the day. Although she wore a knit hat on her head to cover her hair and her face was still smudged with her muddy disguise, I had no trouble deciphering her feminine features.

She lifted her gaze, and at the sight of my face her eyes widened in recognition and my name slipped from her lips. "Collin."

"Lord Collin," I said, unable to resist teasing her. "I thought we got my title straightened out this morning."

"Oh, forgive me, Your Majesty."

I grinned, appreciating the jaunty curve of her lips. "You're forgiven, sweetheart."

Her eyes rounded even more. Was she surprised I'd discovered she wasn't the boy she pretended to be?

"And exactly why are you kidnapping me, Your Majesty?" she said while rapidly regaining her composure. "Did you want to give me another ring?"

I laughed softly, enjoying the witty banter altogether too much.

"Or perhaps this time you're planning to give me real treasure—a pouch of gold or something that might be truly beneficial."

"And who exactly will be benefitting from my gifts?" I watched the moonlight shift across her face.

"People who need it much more than you." Her voice turned hard, and her eyes suddenly glittered, reminding me that she was a thief. If her performance that morning was any indication of her skill, she was good at what she did. Of course she wasn't good enough to elude me, but good nonetheless.

I braced my leg against hers to prevent her from giving me a surprise kick or knee.

"The people on my land aren't suffering," I said.

"And when is the last time you stepped into one of their homes and spoke with them?"

Her question stopped my easy retort. When was the last time I'd spoken to one of the tradesmen who lived in the town bordering my castle, or one of the many peasant farmers who worked my land?

"My point exactly," she said with a smug smile.

"And a good point it is."

At my words of agreement, her smile faltered.

I couldn't keep my grin from widening. For the first time since I'd arrived home, I felt alive. Maybe what I'd needed was a challenge to chase away the boredom and restlessness that had beset me of late. Locating this girl and her accomplice had certainly been a challenge, one I'd thoroughly enjoyed.

Bantering with her in the middle of the forest was also certainly more fun than sitting at another long feast or dancing with one more guest I didn't know or care about.

Upon seeing the dry, mud-caked crease that appeared on her forehead, I could tell she wasn't finding quite as much pleasure in our encounter. "So if you're not planning to lavish me with more of your gifts, why have you kidnapped me?"

"I haven't kidnapped you," I protested, but weakly. After all, I had secured her weapons, silenced her, and dragged her away from her friend. It wasn't exactly the kind of behavior the Noblest Knight had trained me to exhibit.

She lifted a brow, which made the dried mud on her forehead crack even further.

"I was only detaining you," I explained hurriedly, "so that I could learn why you were on my land, stealing from me."

"And I told you. I'm helping people." Her muscles tensed beneath my grip. She was getting ready to attempt her escape.

I strengthened my hold. Her wrists were delicate and my larger, coarser fingers encircled both easily.

"Now that you know my motivation," she said, "you may let me go."

"Oh, may I?" There was something about her way of speaking that didn't fit with her peasant disguise. She was no peasant. But who was she?

"Very well, sweetheart," I said softly. "I'll let you go."

Her lips stalled, likely in surprise at my easy acquiescence.

"But first," I continued, "I want to do this." With a swift jerk, I dislodged her knit cap. Waves of curly hair tumbled down about her face.

She gave a yelp and yanked her hands, trying to free them from my unyielding clutch. For a moment, she twisted and tugged, attempting to pull away.

"Calm down," I said. "I knew you were a girl within seconds of your attack this morning."

Her thrashing came to an abrupt halt. "You did?"

"Of course." I let my gaze linger on the wild curls flowing in abandon over her shoulders and falling halfway down her back. "You're too pretty to be a boy."

She stared at me, her mouth hanging open, her brown eyes dark and wide.

The wind swayed a branch overhead. Moonlight slanted down onto her head for an instant, long enough for me to catch a glint of . . .red?

I stared at the curls, and my mind spun with the revelation. Who was this girl? I studied her face again. I had the feeling I should know her, but I couldn't place from where.

She cocked a brow, as if waiting for me to remember who she was. News of my return had spread far and wide, throughout my lands and beyond. Of course she would identify me. But I had no reason to recognize her, did I?

"Have we met before?" I asked.

She started to nod, but then quickly shook her head. "It's of no consequence." She yanked at her hands once more. "Now let me go."

A shaft of moonlight touched her bare head again, revealing the red of her hair—a blond red the shade of ripening strawberries.

Strawberries.

At the image a vivid memory flashed into my mind, a picture of a little girl in an angelic gown sitting upon a pure white pony. Her red curls had swirled around her pretty face.

It wasn't the first time I'd noticed this girl. My father had always made a point of seeking out Lord Wessex and his red-haired daughter. But the last time, when she'd been on her white pony, had been different, and the memory had stayed with me all those years.

I'd been hunting with my father when we'd chanced upon our neighbors out for a ride. My father then stopped to converse with the lord about issues that didn't interest me.

All I'd cared about that day was the beautiful white pony. More than anything else in the world, I'd wanted to take the pony for a ride. I hadn't cared about the girl who sat atop it, or the fact it wasn't proper etiquette to ask for a ride. I'd sidled next to her and asked her anyway.

I'd been disappointed when she'd refused my request.

And then, in my immaturity, what had I told her? My mind scrambled to remember the insult. Something about her hair being as red as strawberries.

She'd taken it for the insult I'd intended, reached over, slapped my cheek, and then called me a straw-headed hay bale.

I'd just grinned, finding amusement in her anger, which had only made her all the angrier. She'd kicked me in the shin with one of her dainty boots and had earned a stern rebuke from her father.

Her father, the late Lord of Wessex.

For a moment I struggled to remember her given name. But after retracing the steps to my past, I finally found it. Juliana.

She was Juliana Wessex.

Inwardly, a tight coil unraveled. I'd solved the mystery that had puzzled me since I'd seen her that morning. I released one of her hands from my prison-like hold, and lifted my fingers to her tangled curls. "I like strawberries."

She sucked in a breath.

I trailed the spiral down to her shoulder. "In fact, strawberries are my favorite fruit."

Our gazes collided with a force that left me strangely breathless. From the stillness of her chest, I could tell she'd ceased breathing too.

"So, Lady Julianna of Wessex, do you still have your pretty white pony?" I brushed one of her curls off her cheek, inadvertently grazing her skin.

She released her breath, and the warmth of it doused my wrist.

I had the urge to caress her cheek again but instead kept my finger on the curl, tucking it back with the others.

She brought her top teeth down over her lip, nibbled it, and glanced away. "You're mistaken. I'm not Lady Juliana."

In the brief discussion about the late Lord Wessex, Irene had indicated that Charles's only child had perished too. I hadn't thought much of it at the time, especially since it had all happened while I'd been away, and there was nothing I could do any more. Through the darkness, I narrowed my eyes upon the young woman standing before me. I'd only been a boy of eight the last time I'd seen her. After we'd ridden away from Lord Wessex and his daughter, my father had berated me and told me a good son wouldn't have thrown away the opportunity to form a match with the girl. He had always envied the neighboring lands, and often schemed ways he could gain them through such a union. One week later, my father had disciplined me for my failure by sending me to live with the Duke of Rivenshire.

I'd only blamed Juliana for a few days. It hadn't taken me long to realize how privileged I was to live in the duke's household as a page. Juliana's kick in the shins had actually turned into the best thing that had happened to me. I owed her my gratitude.

Even though she was now grown and shadowed by the night, I had no doubt this thief and Juliana Wessex were one and the same person. But she obviously didn't want me to know that fact.

"What became of Lady Juliana?" I asked.

"She died in a peasant uprising." The answer was too quick, almost bitter.

"And you still haven't told me—what happened to her pretty white pony?"

Juliana stared off into the dark forest, refusing to meet my gaze. "It was riddled with so many arrows, it turned crimson as it bled to death."

"Blessed Mary." The low tightness of her voice reached into my chest and clutched my heart.

Her eyes glistened and she chewed at her bottom lip again.

I slid my hand to her shoulder. "I'm sorry, Juliana."

She nodded, and her chin slowly sank so that I was left looking at the top of her bare head.

I fingered another one of her curls. I wasn't sure what the real story was behind the death of Charles Wessex, but I could sense there was much more to it than either Juliana or Irene had told me. And I would find out every detail, eventually.

Throwing away all caution, I released Juliana's wrists and tugged her forward, so that she stood only inches from me. I knew we were practically strangers, that even when we'd been children we'd only known each other in passing. Even so, there was something vulnerable in her stance that made me want to protect her and right the wrongs she had endured.

I ignored the warning clamoring through my mind, reminding me that she was disguised as a thief and that she'd robbed me only that morning. Instead, I reached for her other shoulder and squeezed it, hoping she could sense my offer of friendship.

She held herself stiffly for a moment before she slumped, as if the weight of all her sorrows and pains had fallen upon her in that moment.

"Whatever's going on, Juliana, I'll help you," I whispered, knowing I could do nothing less. "I promise."

At my words, she tensed and took a step away. "I don't need your help, Collin."

"I want to—"

"I'm faring well enough." She straightened.

"Oh, is that what you call this?" I asked. "Getting kidnapped in the middle of the night?"

Her features hardened, and all traces of sadness dissipated.

"If this is faring well," I said, "then I dread to see what bad looks like."

"You won't have to see." She glared at me. "I'm good at what I do. In fact, I'm the best in the land."

"The best thief?"

"As a matter of fact, yes."

"I suppose that's why I caught you? Because you're so good?" I grinned at her stubbornness. It was all I could think to do at the absurdity of the situation.

"I most certainly don't need you around, mocking me as you're wont to do." She took another step backward.

"I'm not mocking you. I simply find you humorous."

"Well, maybe you won't find me so humorous once I escape." With that, she sprang away.

I chuckled and started after her. I liked her spunk.

In the darkness I could hear her crashing through the brush, making as much noise as a mother bear pursuing an enemy. I started after her, following with little effort the path she was blazing.

Somehow she managed to stay several steps ahead, her lithe body racing through the brush as if it were an open field. After several minutes my lungs began to ache from the speed of the chase. She was fast, and I was surprised that she could keep going without slowing down. If my lungs were burning, I knew hers were too.

Finally, when I wasn't sure I could go on, I heard her crash. I stumbled to a halt. For a long moment, the forest was silent around me. I crouched low behind a trunk and tried to peer through the blackness to locate her.

After a few seconds of searching in the faint moonlight, I located her outline in a beech tree several paces away.

I had to admit, she was no bumbling idiot. She knew what she was doing.

But in the stillness of the forest, questions shouted through my mind. As Charles Wessex's only child and heir, why was she living in the forest as a thief? My sister and others believed Juliana had died with her father. And since she was living under disguise, Juliana apparently wished no one to know she was in fact alive.

But why?

Part of me said I should do the honorable thing and walk away from her. If she wanted to remain hidden and continue her thieving lifestyle, who was I to interfere?

But another part of me wanted to help her, even if she claimed she didn't want my aid. Deep in my gut, I knew it was only a matter of time before she got caught—no matter how skilled she might be. And I dreaded to think what might happen to her.

In fact, if I'd been someone more sinister—a lusty man without any regard for her womanhood—what would she have done tonight? If I could easily discover she was a woman, surely with time someone else would as well.

I swallowed hard, letting determination push aside my misgivings. I wouldn't let her escape, not until I had answers to the many questions that were rampaging through me.

With a stealth I'd developed during the many battles I'd fought with the duke, I climbed into the tree closest to me. Several of the larger limbs intertwined with the beech, where Juliana was hiding on a low branch that formed a V with the trunk. I slowly slipped from one tree to the next, until I was slightly above her. The cover of the leaves hid me, and the soft rattle of the wind through the branches muffled my steps. In the shadows of the limbs and changing leaves, she was perched and ready to spring. She peered down, likely searching the ground around the tree for me.

Finally, I lowered myself, unfolding my lean frame next to hers. "Looking for me?" I whispered.

She gave a start and straightened quickly—too quickly. She wobbled and flailed her arms. Before I could grab her, she fell backward off the branch and plunged toward the earth.

A small yelp was followed by a thwack and then a thump.

My heart sped with sudden panic. "Juliana?"

Complete silence greeted me and pushed the anxiety into my blood. I jumped after her. The drop wasn't far and I landed on my feet, the impact jarring my knees only a little.

"Juliana?" I called louder, searching the base of the tree.

Moonlight touched on the red-gold of her hair, now tangled in the brush and leaves.

My heartbeat slammed to a halt. "Blessed Mary." I scrambled toward her. She lay unmoving, her hair sprawled around her pale face.

I touched her lips with my fingertips and drew in a shaky breath at the moist air she released.

She was alive.

My hands slid gently to her limbs, searching for broken bones, gashes, or any other sign of distress. As I probed and felt the thinness of her body, I swallowed back dismay. She was too gaunt, the hungry-thin I'd seen on siege victims who'd slowly starved to death.

I touched her head, and she gave a soft moan. I probed the back of her skull until I found a slick spot of blood.

She must have hit her head during the fall.

I gently slipped my hands under her body. What had I been thinking to chase her around the forest in the dead of the night? Why hadn't I been more careful?

The whole escapade may have brought me the rush of excitement that had been eluding me since I'd returned home. But at what cost?

I was a selfish fool and I should have put an end to the chase sooner.

I lifted her with the care I'd give a rare jewel. As far as I could tell, her only injury was the knock she'd taken to her head during the fall. But I wouldn't be sure until I'd checked her more thoroughly. And to do that, I'd have to take her back to my home. I most certainly couldn't leave her out in the forest injured.

I shifted her into my arms, cradling her like a babe against my chest.

Her body was limp and her head lolled back. As I started back through the forest to my horse, she didn't utter a word.

"I'm sorry, Juliana," I whispered.

I knew with certainty she would have protested had she known where I was taking her. But what other choice did I have?

# Chapter 5

*From the softness that surrounded me, I could almost* believe I was floating upon a cloud. The warmth was heavenly, as if sun poured over me and wrapped me in its solid beams.

I sighed and soaked in the delight of my fairy-tale world. I hadn't been so warm and comfortable since . . . My mind stumbled to remember a time.

Then it came to me. I hadn't experienced such comfort since I'd been a little girl, in the days when I'd lived with my father in Wessex Castle. I'd had chambers of my own, a big, canopied bed, and servants to wait on me.

Strange I would imagine this now, after so many years of the cold, hard earth serving as my bed. I stretched, still dreaming of warm coverlets snuggled around my body and feather pillows piled beneath my head.

My stomach rumbled, urging me to wake from my dream. The gnawing hunger was the signal I needed to begin my daily routine of hunting, not for myself but for all the other bellies that relied upon my game.

The waft of something roasting sent another gurgle into my stomach. I sniffed and dragged in the delicious scents of fresh-baked bread and venison stew.

"Has she awoken?" a voice drifted into my dream.

Suddenly, I wished more than anything to stay asleep. I was in the best dream I'd ever had, and I didn't want it to end.

A cool hand pressed against my forehead, and then gentle fingers brushed my hair back.

"Father," I whispered, an ache forming in my chest. The last time my father had touched my hair, he'd been bleeding to death on a pallet in a peasant hut. His blood had bubbled out of his wounds, spilling onto the dirt floor, forming into mud. Though my uncle's army was approaching, to capture Father for the final time, his cool fingers, sticky with blood, had caressed my forehead, wiped the tears from my cheeks, and then had combed the tangles out of my face.

The fingers caressed my hair again. "Juliana?"

The voice was definitely not my father's.

A rush of memories flooded my conscience, memories of running through the forest, of climbing a tree, and then falling. The rush was followed by a burst of terror.

My eyes flew open to the sight of a golden canopy hanging above me. My gaze shifted to the face hovering near mine. A handsome face covered with a couple days' worth of scruff. A lock of blond hair fell over a creased forehead. And worried green eyes peered down at me.

"Collin Goodrich?" I asked. "What are you doing here?" Why was he a part of my dreams?

At my question, his lips curved into a smile that made my stomach do a funny flip.

"You're awake," he said, bringing his hand to my cheek and making a gentle path down to my chin.

"Why are you here?" I asked through the grogginess in my throat, letting myself stare at him.

He seemed to be doing the same with my face, his gaze making a leisurely trail from my cheek to my chin to my lips, until the brilliant green finally met my eyes again. The lightness and warmth there seeped into me and spread through my middle.

"I'm here because I live here," he said.

The words slapped me fully awake and brought back all my memories. I'd robbed him, and then he'd tracked me down and dragged me away from Thatch. And now he'd brought me back to his castle?

I fought down a panicked cry, shoved away the coverlet, and pushed myself off the ultra-soft feather mattress. I climbed out of the bed and was on my feet before Collin could rise from the chair positioned next to me.

Fierce, blinding pain rammed through my head, almost as if a blacksmith was banging his anvil against my skull. I swayed, black dizziness threatening to make me collapse.

Collin jumped to his feet and reached for me before my knees gave way. I was helpless to do anything but sag against him, my body weak, my legs unable to support my weight, and my head pounding.

For a moment I leaned into him, remembering the few seconds in the forest when he'd comforted me even when I hadn't known I'd needed it.

What was there about this man that made me feel like I'd gained a friend, when I knew he was nothing more than the enemy? I straightened and tugged away from him. I couldn't forget who he was and what he represented.

He let me step back but still held onto my arms, keeping me from toppling over.

"You brought me to your home?" The words came out a strangled whisper. For the first time I glanced around the spacious chamber, taking in the luxurious tapestries covering the walls, the wide stone hearth ablaze with a glowing fire, the enormous canopied bed, and the heavy curtains.

A short, stoop-shouldered servant stood in front of an open wardrobe, her hand poised on a gown she'd been about to hang with the assortment of other glorious garments.

My panic swelled. What if the servant recognized me? What if word reached my uncle that I was still alive?

I had the overwhelming urge to plunge back into the bed and pull the coverlet over my head. Instead I broke free of Collin and lurched toward the door, my footsteps unsteady like those of a babe just learning to walk.

All I could think was that I needed to get away. Now. I had to get back into the forest and hide before anyone figured out who I really was.

"Wait," Collin called.

I forced my legs to move faster and fixed my attention on the door, which seemed a league away. If I could make my way outside the walls of the castle, I would find Thatch and he would help me. But I only made it halfway across the room before my legs gave way, and I crashed to the rushes strewn over the cold floor.

In an instant, Collin was at my side. Amidst my weak cry of protest, he slid his arms underneath me and lifted my body effortlessly.

"And where exactly do you think you're running off to?"

"As far away as possible," I whispered.

He tucked me against his chest, and I loathed myself for laying my head against him and relishing the comfort of his hold.

"You can't go anywhere yet," he chided into my ear. "Not wearing only a nightgown."

Only then did I realize someone had divested me of my tunic and breeches and had dressed me in a thick linen night-dress. The soft garment covered me from my neck to my toes. Even so, hot embarrassment pulsed through me.

Had Collin changed my clothes?

He chuckled. "No, sweetheart," he whispered in answer to my unspoken question. "I had Mistress Higgins change and bathe you." He nodded in the direction of the servant at the wardrobe. The woman bowed slightly. The gorget surrounding her throat and the tight veil covering her head left only her face exposed, an aged face that was as wrinkled and cracked as a parched field. But her eyes were soft pools, which regarded me kindly.

"Bathe?" I squeaked the word.

This time Collin gave a full, hearty laugh. "Even though you were quite pretty covered in mud, you're absolutely stunning without it."

At his lavish compliment, fresh warmth coursed through me, and I was tempted to hide my face in his tunic. But I forced myself to meet his gaze instead. "You had no right to bring me here."

"I had no other choice." His eyes held an apology. "You've been unconscious for the past two days."

"Two days?"

"Don't worry. You're safe." He stopped at the edge of the bed. "I've told everyone that you're a friend who was traveling to visit me, but you were attacked on your way."

I couldn't keep from admiring the strength and ease with which he held me, as if I were nothing more than that girl of five. "At least it's not a complete lie," I said dryly. "I *was* attacked."

"I'm sorry." His grin faded. "I never meant for you to get hurt." His face was near mine, his eyes honest, the regret in his expression palpable.

I was suddenly breathless. I'd never been in such close proximity to a man, and I was quite sure if my father had been there, he wouldn't have been pleased with the situation. Nevertheless, I couldn't bring myself to make Collin put me down. Yet.

"It wasn't your fault," I admitted. "I was entirely too careless. And it won't happen again."

"Well, that's good to hear."

"Next time, you won't get near me."

"There doesn't have to be a next time." His expression was much too serious, and he made no effort to hide his frank appreciation.

He wasn't merely flattering me with his compliments about my appearance. He really did like how I looked.

I squirmed, not quite sure how to handle that revelation. I doubted many of my companions even counted me as a woman. Bulldog had insisted I take a man's disguise before he let me ride with him, and I'd kept the front ever since. Not only did I dress like a man, but I acted like one and fought better than most. My one vanity was my hair. Even though Bulldog had suggested that I cut it, I hadn't been able to.

This interaction with Collin, this obvious awareness of each other, was entirely new to me. For the first time in my life, I realized I was no longer a young girl. I was becoming a woman.

"I think you'd better put me down," I said.

He didn't immediately release me—instead a slow grin worked its way up his lips, as if he'd sensed the direction of my thoughts. "Only if you promise that you'll stay and let me help you in whatever trouble you've gotten yourself into."

"I won't promise that at all. Now put me down."

"Can't you forgive me for the childishness of my past?" He fingered a strand of my hair. "I was an idiot. I love your hair. It's absolutely the most beautiful color in the world."

My insides fluttered at his lavish praise—praise I wasn't accustomed to receiving. I twisted in his arms, knowing I had to put a safe distance between us. The motion forced him to lower me back to the mattress.

I quickly dragged the coverlet over myself and stared up at him.

He cocked his brow. "Well?"

I glanced at Mistress Higgins by the wardrobe. She'd discreetly turned her humped back on us and was arranging the gowns.

"Mistress Higgins is one of my most trusted servants," Collin reassured. "She served as a lady's maid to my mother, and you have nothing to fear from her."

I pursed my lips and crossed my arms. Surely he didn't think I was foolish enough to speak of my past in front of strangers.

Collin flopped down into his chair and reclined as though he didn't have a care in the world. "Very well. Mistress Higgins, will you be so kind as to give me a moment of privacy with our guest?"

The lady's maid hesitated, glancing from Collin to me and back.

Even though I lived and slept around men all of the time, Mistress Higgins insinuation made me realize that in this setting, in the world of the nobility, it would be entirely improper for me to be left unchaperoned with Collin. As if recognizing the same, Collin cocked his head at the door. "If you wouldn't mind leaving the door open and waiting just outside?"

She nodded, curtsied, and once she'd left us alone, Collin slipped from his chair and kneeled beside me. "Forgive me? I beg of you to forgive me and put me out of my misery."

Something inside me wanted to reassure him. His charm made him almost irresistible. But I only had to think of Thatch, who'd been homeless for years, and Bulldog, who'd lost his thumbs trying to keep his son from starving to death, and all thoughts of peace with Collin Goodrich fled.

"I'll think about forgiving you for my childish grudge," I said. "But you're a nobleman. And I can't ever forgive you for that."

"What do you have against noblemen? Your father was one. And apparently you've forgotten that *you* are of noble birth too."

"I've cut myself off from that lifestyle and will never rejoin it." The resentment that had grown inside me over the past several years rose swiftly. "I loathe it and everything it stands for."

Other than a raised brow, he didn't seem surprised by my outburst. In fact, if anything, the twinkle in his eye spoke of his amusement. "All the more reason to stay a week and let me prove that you don't need to loathe me."

"A week won't change anything." Although the tantalizing scents of bread and stew coming in through the open doorway of the chamber had grown stronger and beckoned me to stay too.

"I dare you to try." His eyes narrowed in provocation, and the muscles in his face tightened.

Something in his expression irked me, as if he didn't believe I would be able to rise to his challenge.

"You're afraid you'll end up liking me by the end of the week," he said.

"I won't."

"Oh yes, you will."

"No, I won't."

He grinned too self-confidently but didn't argue further.

"Besides, even if I wanted to take you up on your challenge," I said, "too many people rely upon me. If I'm not there, they'll go hungry."

"I'm sure they'll be fine without you. You'll have to stay for a few more days anyway, until you're stronger and steadier on your feet."

I shook my head. If he wouldn't let me leave now, I'd wait for the cover of darkness and sneak out. By now, Thatch would be frantic with worry about what had happened to me. I had to get to him and reassure him I was fine.

Collin reached into his cloak and pulled out a red velvet pouch. He patted the bulge against his palm, creating a distinct jangle. "Will you stay if I promise you a purse of gold at the week's end?"

A purse of gold? My heart pattered fast at the thought of how many sacks of grain that would buy, and how much wool for spinning toward socks and mittens.

"What do you want in return?"

"Just one week of your time to prove that I'm not as despicable as you think I am. Be an honored guest in my home this week. Let me entertain you." He nodded toward the open wardrobe. "And maybe wear one or two of those gowns."

"Do you promise not to reveal my true identity?"

"I promise. As far as everyone else is concerned, you're merely an old friend who's come for a visit."

I narrowed my eyes. He was right. My companions could survive a week without me. Bulldog and some of the other men would be able to find the game they needed. And if I swallowed my pride and stayed a week with Collin, I would be able to ride away with enough gold to feed my friends through the upcoming winter without having to resort to any more stealing.

How could I refuse the offer?

Maybe this was my chance to do something truly beneficial for all the people who depended upon me. Maybe I'd even have the chance to show Collin the error of his extravagant ways, to show him the reality of how much the peasants were suffering. In fact . . .

"If I accept your challenge to stay here in your castle with you for a week and act the part of a noblewoman," I said slowly, my mind spinning with a new plan, "will you accept my challenge to stay with me in the forest for a week and play the part of a peasant?"

"Of course." He responded eagerly, as if I'd just invited him to a party.

"You'll have to leave your wealth behind."

"Sounds fun."

I clenched my fingers into a fist. "Living as a peasant is the furthest thing from fun you can imagine." He was impossibly spoiled and pampered. All the more reason to drag him into my forest home and let him see firsthand the deprivation and squalor that threaded every aspect of our lives.

"I'm ready for the challenge." His arrogant expression only aggravated me more. "But I'm not sure that you are."

I pushed myself up on the feather mattress so that I was sitting. The pounding in my head returned with blinding force. The idea of acting like a noblewoman repulsed me, quite literally made me want to vomit.

But I couldn't back down now, not with that purse of gold awaiting me. And not with the opportunity to humble Collin Goodrich and expose him to the sad reality of life for altogether too many people.

I met his gaze head on. "Bring me one of the gowns."

A slow smile spread over his lips. "Then it's a deal?"

"Yes, you have yourself a deal."

# Chapter
## 6

*Mistress Higgins bound the last lace at the side of* the gown and then stood back and smiled, the movement adding more deep grooves to her wrinkled face. "Lovely. Just lovely."

I stared down at the folds of luxurious teal satin that swished around me. An equally lavish kirtle of gold damask showed through the slits down the sides of the skirt.

"Just look at you." Miss Higgins held up a mirror.

I shook my head and turned away. "I trust that you've done a good job, Mistress Higgins."

The lady's maid had spent the past hour dressing me in many layers of garments and arranging my hair so that it was fashionably plaited on the top of my head. With each passing minute, my stomach had cinched tighter until it was ready to spring shut like one of my traps.

I eyed the open, arched window again as I had a hundred times since Mistress Higgins had started her ministrations. 'Twas no fault of the servant's. The lady's maid had been angelic. If I didn't know better, I'd have guessed Collin handpicked his kindest servant to be my maid during my weeklong stay.

Even so, I was growing more anxious to make my escape and fly like an arrow as far away as I could. But I'd made a deal with Collin, and I couldn't break it after just one day, could I?

I fidgeted with the scooped neckline that revealed far more skin than I was accustomed to in my men's tunics.

After spending yesterday resting and recovering from my head injury, I'd finally risen that morning. Even though my head still ached, I'd been too restless to stay abed any longer. So I'd agreed to Collin's invitation to join him and the other guests in the Great Hall for dinner.

I had been tempted to hide in my room for the length of my stay. But a driving need prodded me to prove to Collin that I could handle anything he might ask me to do. I had to show him that none of his efforts could sway my dislike of the nobility.

But now that I was attired in the extravagant gown, with my hair piled on top of my head, I didn't know if I could go through with the bargain.

A soft rap upon the door sent a bolt of panic through me. "Is Lady Eleanora ready?" came Collin's voice from the hallway.

Collin had decided to call me Lady Eleanora Delacroix, after one of his childhood friends, a lady he'd known while living in the service of the Duke of Rivenshire. Since I was already accustomed to living under the guise of the Cloaked Bandit, I could surely play the part of someone new. I only hoped none of the other guests would know the real Eleanora.

Mistress Higgins started toward the door. Her footsteps, like the rest of her demeanor, were saintly. She was plain, with straight gray hair beneath her veil, and an austere tunic. She almost looked as though she belonged in a convent instead of a castle.

I glanced again with longing at the window. Had Thatch figured out who had captured me? That Lord Goodrich had tracked us down after our theft? Whether he knew or not, he'd probably returned to Bulldog with the news of my captivity. Somehow, I would need to send them word that I was alive and faring well.

Mistress Higgins swung the door wide. Collin stepped into the room holding one hand behind his back. The swirling teal-and-gold pattern of his tunic and trousers matched my garments, almost as if he'd planned it that way.

As my lady's maid stepped aside to reveal me, his ready grin disappeared and was replaced by astonishment, his greeting stalling into an open-mouthed stare.

My fingers fluttered first to my neckline and then to the tiny dangle of curls next to my ear. "Is something wrong?"

Collin closed his mouth and then swallowed hard.

"I can't ever remember a time when Lord Collin was speechless," Mistress Higgins said with a knowing smile.

"Perhaps I should have chanced a glance in the mirror." I took a step back. "I can only imagine how utterly silly I must look—"

"No," Collin cut in, finally finding his voice. "You don't look silly at all. Far from it . . ." His attention shifted downward, taking in every inch from the neckline to the way the gown hugged my waist and then flared into a bell shape as it cascaded into a glossy river on the floor behind me. When his gaze lifted and met mine, awe rounded his eyes and revealed stark admiration shining in their depths.

I clasped my hands to hold back a tremble. I needed to stop acting like a spooked mare.

Collin started toward me, the rushes muting his steps. My heart thudded louder until I was sure he could hear it. He didn't stop until he stood directly in front of me. "You are stunning, my lady."

Warmth pulsed through me, sending tingles to my toes, which were squeezed into long-pointed poulaines. I didn't know why his words should delight me so much, but they did. More than I wanted to admit.

He leaned closer until his mouth was near my ear. "You're so beautiful, Juliana," he whispered, his breath brushing against the sensitive skin at the pulse in my neck.

At his nearness, the air caught in my lungs.

When he pulled back, the green of his eyes held none of the usual mirth.

I didn't know what to do. My own body betrayed me by reacting to him, by noticing how handsome he was too, enjoying his compliments, and wishing he'd whisper in my ear again.

"So I'm acceptable then?" I stepped away from him and tried to harden my voice. "Do I pass your test?" I had to stay in control. I couldn't let him sway me with his dazzling eyes and sweet words.

He reached for one of my hands, not letting me escape. A slow smile spread and the light in his eyes told me he could see past my gruffness. "You passed my test even when you wore a man's tunic."

He brought his other hand out from behind his back and held out a necklace. It was simple but elegant, a single strand of diamonds with a larger teardrop diamond at the center. "For you."

I held back a gasp. "I refuse to wear anything so extravagant—"

"I want you to have it," he said softly.

I shook my head. "I can't."

"Please." His eyes pleaded with me.

I couldn't make myself look at the necklace again. It was pretty, prettier than anything I'd worn since—since the days when I'd dressed up for parties with my father. He'd always delighted in showering me with jewels and gifts, surprising me with tokens of his affection.

At the memory, an ache lodged in my chest. Those had been peaceful days, filled with such joy. My father and I had always had such fun together, just the two of us. Until the day Uncle had ridden into our lives . . .

Collin leaned in and lowered his voice so that Mistress Higgins, near the door, couldn't hear him. "At the end of the week, you can keep all the jewels I give you."

How could I resist? Not only would I walk away with a purse of gold, but I'd have the necklace too. "Very well," I said, holding out my hand. "I'll wear it, but only because of what it will provide to those in need at the week's end."

He didn't place it into my hand, but instead held it up to my neck. "May I?" He indicated that I should turn around and allow him to put it on me.

My stomach quivered and I rotated quickly, not wanting him to see my reaction.

He draped the necklace around my throat. The silver was cold and heavy against my skin, but his fingers at the back of my neck were as soft as the feathers of a baby bird. Working at the clasp, he faltered and brushed the skin where tiny, loose curls had refused submission into the knot Mistress Higgins had wound upward on my head.

I sucked in a breath at the contact.

He finished tightening the links, but didn't immediately pull away. His fingers lingered on the chain with the edges barely grazing my skin. A warm burst of his breath hovered above my neck.

I held myself still, hardly daring to breathe. What was happening to me? Now that I was dressed as a woman, was I beginning to feel like one too? Perhaps I'd acted the part of a man for so long that I'd forgotten what it was like to even be a woman.

I nibbled at my lip and then spun away from him, toward the door, toward Mistress Higgins—who still wore a secretive smile, as if she knew more about what was occurring between Collin and me than either of us could understand.

"I'm not sure I should show you off tonight," Collin said once he'd caught up to me in the hallway. He offered me his arm and the look in his eyes smoldered. "I'd almost rather keep you to myself."

I knew I ought to slip my hand into the crook of his arm and accept his gentlemanly offer of assistance, but I pretended not to notice. The merest contact with him was doing funny things to my composure, and if I hoped to survive the evening, I needed to be more careful.

"I'd prefer to stay off to the side, out of the way," I said as we neared the entrance of the Great Hall. "The less attention I draw to myself, the safer I'll be."

"You don't really think anyone will recognize you as the Cloaked Bandit, do you?" Collin whispered with a mischievous grin.

"Of course they won't." I feigned nonchalance. Even if Collin had figured out who I really was, I wouldn't admit it, even to him. "They won't consider such a thing, because it's absolutely ridiculous and untrue."

He laughed. "You're absolutely fascinating."

I didn't have time to consider what the tone of his voice meant or the look in his eye, before he ushered me into the spacious hall. The other guests were already mingling, laughing, and chattering, and thankfully hardly noticed our entrance.

The servants bustled about carrying ale and wine, refilling goblets. The minstrels were playing. And rich aromas of roasted fowl, almond pudding, and spiced apple tarts wafted through the air, coming from the hallway that led to the kitchen. My mouth watered at the thought of tasting an apple tart. It had been years since I'd had anything so fine or sweet.

The long room was like the Great Hall of Wessex Castle, with a vaulted ceiling and oblong stained glass windows providing some light in the fading evening. But the decorations that graced the room were much more elaborate, the tapestries rich and complex, and the colors more vibrant.

Collin Goodrich was indeed a wealthy man, and his family had always made sure everyone knew their status. His father had been among the neighbors who had turned a blind eye to all that my uncle had done to my father. He'd ignored my father's plea for help when my uncle had first arrived with his army and pack of lies. Although my father had never said why the Goodriches hadn't come to our aid, I'd guessed it had to do with the fact that the late Lord Goodrich had held a grudge against my father because he hadn't agreed to the liaison that Collin's father had wanted between myself and Collin.

As we were seated at the front table, Collin carried on a lively stream of conversation with the guests around him and attempted to include me. He even introduced me to his sister, whom I recognized as the lady present in Collin's hunting party when I'd robbed him earlier in the week.

I didn't realize how nervous I was until halfway through the main course, when my heart finally subsided to its normal rhythm. I wasn't at all surprised when the servants brought out a peacock that had been cooked and then reassembled with its feathers. Or when they delivered a pastry molded into the shape of a miniature castle.

All the while I ate of the peacock—along with roasted swans, geese, and heron—my thoughts drifted to Thatch and Bulldog and the others huddled together in the cold fall air, their bellies rumbling from hunger. The ewerer brought us basins of water between courses. As I rinsed, I couldn't stop looking at my hands, scrubbed free of the dirt that had become a way of life, or thinking of how my friends and I usually devoured every morsel of food and licked our fingers clean afterward.

The warmth, the laughter, the unending dishes of food surrounded me and made me dizzy with reminders of my former life, which had been so cruelly wrenched away. The ache in my heart swelled painfully. If only my father had been less trusting . . . then perhaps he would still be alive and I would have been sitting in my own Great Hall dining with him.

Tears burned the back of my eyes. I pushed away from the table and stood.

Collin stopped in the middle of the conversation he was having with the man next to him and turned to me, his brow creasing.

"I need a breath of air," I said. "If you'll excuse me."

Without waiting for his permission or his reaction, I made my escape out a side door. A harried scullion boy pointed me in the direction of the kitchen, which I knew would eventually lead me to an exit.

I ducked into the busy kitchen, ignoring the stares of the servants who stopped stirring and cutting and basting to watch me race to the door. The blood from the butchering slickened the floor, along with feathers, and entrails the dogs hadn't yet cleaned up. The heat from the two fireplaces dampened my forehead, so that when I finally burst free through the outer door, the cool evening air soothed my face.

I plunged forward into the darkness of the orchard and gardens that surrounded the kitchen entrance and pushed aside my melancholy and guilt over the fact I'd halfway enjoyed the meal and wished to be eating it in my own Great Hall. Instead I tried to be angry, to return my thoughts to all the injustices I'd witnessed, especially the disparity between the nobility and the poor.

I'd learned over the years that 'twas always better to be angry than sad.

Besides, how had I ever lived in such opulence? So calloused, so unconcerned for those people who had nothing? Who went to bed every night cold and hungry?

Even the lowest kitchen maid here had a better life than I had living in the forest.

"Jul—Lady Eleanora, wait," came Collin's soft call behind me.

I didn't stop but sped deeper into the orchard, the tangy scent of overripe apples filling each labored breath. His footsteps crunched louder behind mine until his hand finally gripped my arm, forcing me to halt. He lifted his torch high, illuminating my face.

"Leave me alone," I muttered while swiping at the unexpected wetness on my cheeks. Had I been crying? If so, it had been a long time since I'd allowed myself such a luxury. Tears were for weaklings, not for strong women like myself.

Collin didn't release my arm, but instead passed the torch to the servant who had followed him, and he then dragged me closer. "Are you running away already?" His voice hinted at humor.

"If I wanted to run away, I would, and there's nothing you'd be able to do to stop me."

He chuckled, but ceased when he saw my face and the traces of tears lingering in my eyelashes. "You're upset," he said, lifting fingers to my cheeks and touching a tear I'd missed.

I brushed his hand away and wiped at my cheeks again. I glanced at the servant. Collin followed my gaze and then nodded to the man, who proceeded to position himself a discreet distance away.

Once we had a modicum of privacy, I spoke in hushed tones. "I only regret that I've subjected myself to this extravagance when so many of my friends would be satisfied with the crusts of bread left over from the banquet."

"Then we shall send them a banquet of their own. I shall have the cook prepare anything you wish. Tell me what you want, and it shall be so."

I shook my head.

"Anything," he said, pulling me to him, ever so gently.

I couldn't resist the tug. And when his arms closed about me, drawing me into his embrace, I crumpled against him and rested my head on his shoulder as though it fit there.

I didn't know what about him drew me, except that he was kind and concerned about me in a way I hadn't experienced in a long time. Even though Bulldog cared about me as fiercely as if I were his own daughter, he never hugged me. He expected me to be tough, like a man. And I always had been.

But with Collin . . . He had a way about him—a tenderness—that seemed to break through the hard walls I'd built around myself.

I nestled my nose against the silkiness of his tunic and breathed in his spicy scent.

His hand cupped the small of my back and pressed me nearer, so that his chin rested against my head. In the short time I'd known him, it hadn't taken me long to realize he was kinder and sweeter than any man I'd ever known. In fact, he reminded me of my father. Had my father been alive to meet Collin as he was now, I was sure he would have liked him—perhaps even a great deal. Maybe he even would have agreed to the union Collin's father had wanted, and would have gained an ally.

"Tell me what you want me to do, and I'll do it," he whispered again. "I'll do anything for you."

I closed my eyes at the comfort that came from his words. I'd had to be strong for so long. I'd had to fight and scrap and struggle to stay alive. Everyone else depended upon me. And it felt so good to lean on someone else for a change and to know I wasn't alone.

He held me quietly for a long moment. In a distant stable, the baying of a hunting hound rose in the night air. But otherwise, the orchard was silent, and the steady thud of Collin's heart filled me with peace.

What would it be like to stop fighting? To stop thieving? To stop living in the woods? What would it be like to return to a normal life, one where I wasn't hunting every day or being hunted by those who wanted me dead?

I shook my head and pulled back from Collin. "No. There's nothing you can do." I spoke the words sadly at first. But then the hopelessness of my life crashed back into me and renewed my anger. As long as Uncle lived, there was very little chance that my friends or I would ever be able to move out of our secret homes deep in the forest. We would have to hide there for the rest of our days, continuing to find ways to survive as best we could.

Even if Collin sent Bulldog a feast of the grandest proportions, the food would eventually be gone, and we would be left in the same situation we'd been in before—helpless, homeless, and hunted.

Revolt was out of the question. Look where it had gotten Father—he'd been mortally wounded during the uprising he'd led. Friends had brought him back to his hut where I'd been able to say good-bye to him before Bulldog had dragged me away into hiding. I'd heard that not long after our leaving, Father had been captured. Even though he'd been bleeding to death, Uncle's men had still tortured him in the most hideous fashion and tossed the pieces of his bloodied remains into the gutter.

Collin brushed a wisp of hair off my cheek. "There's got to be something I can do to make you happy. Something I can give you."

I wished there was. I wished there was a way to change everything. But the reality was that I would have to return to the forest at the end of the week. And maybe with Collin's purse of gold and the diamond necklace, I wouldn't have to resort to thieving for a while.

"Let's just follow through with our bargains to one another," I said, putting more distance between us. "That's all I want."

If only that really was all I wanted.

# Chapter

## 7

I SIPPED THE WARM ALE AND IGNORED THE LEDGER SPREAD open on the table in front of me. Even though my steward had brought it out upon my request, I couldn't muster any enthusiasm for making sense of the numbers.

Something deep inside admonished me to put forward at least a little energy in gaining a basic understanding of the massive fortune I'd inherited from my father. But now that I was actually sitting in the cozy solar, ready to take more responsibility as I knew I should, I couldn't think of anything but Juliana. The transformation from bandit to beauty had been so complete, she'd taken my breath away. Seeing her in my hall at the banquet, I'd known that's where she belonged. She'd blended in and resumed her natural role as a lady, with an elegance and poise as if she'd never left.

More than that, I couldn't stop thinking about her dedication to her band of thieving followers. The only reason she'd agreed to my bargain was so that she could get the gold— not for herself, but for them. I admired her commitment, her loyalty, and her willingness to sacrifice, even if she was going about it all in the wrong ways.

And I was still marveling that she'd allowed me to comfort her in the garden. Embracing her had made my heart drum with a new kind of desire—a longing to be with her again, to spend the day with her, to discover more about her.

I sighed and stared unseeingly at William's meticulous marks on the parchment pages. "You've done a good job keeping the records, William," I finally said to my steward, who stood next to the desk.

William pushed his thick eyeglasses up on his nose. "Thank you, thank you, my lord. Do you have any questions? Any questions at all?"

"William has kept me quite apprised," Irene piped in from her chair in front of the hearth, where she sat quietly working on her embroidery. "And he's been as frugal and conscientious as he was when father was alive."

William shifted and bumped into the quill pen perched on the corner of the desk. The pen toppled and William fumbled for it, but it slipped through his fingers and clattered to the floor.

I tried to focus on the numbers that filled the neat columns. Even if I understood what all the notes meant, I still wouldn't know what questions to ask.

Juliana's statement in the garden last evening came back to me as it had throughout the long night. *I only regret that I've subjected myself to this extravagance when so many of my friends would be satisfied with the crusts of bread left over from the banquet.*

Did I live in extravagance? Were others suffering while I feasted?

Obviously, the poor farmers and peasants who resided on my land didn't live the way I did. Nor did they expect to. They accepted their position in life the same way I did mine.

Sure, I'd visited among the poor with Lady Rosemarie this past summer. I'd witnessed her compassion. But at the time, I'd assumed they were in need because of the strange plague devastating their towns. But what if the poor were suffering more than I'd ever considered?

"William," I started, trying to work out my confusion. "Can we put together gifts for the poorest tenants on our land?"

"Gifts, my lord?" William had stooped to pick up the quill pen, but at my question it slipped from his fingers and clattered to the floor again.

I leaned back in the stiff chair my father had sat in every day of his life as he counted his gold and poured over the numbers William recorded. "Yes. You know, extra food, clothing, whatever they need."

William opened and then closed his mouth, and then opened it again. The eyeglasses on the end of his nose made his eyes look especially big. They were kind eyes, but also astute.

"Our tenants don't need anything, Collin." Irene peered at me over the tapestry in her hand, her needle poised to execute the next stitch. "They're content and happy. If we send them gifts, they'll only grow to expect more than they need."

I grinned. "So you think we'll spoil them?"

She didn't return my smile. "I think we treat the people on our land more kindly than most. And our kindness is gift enough."

I was tempted to shrug off the entire discussion. My idea had only been a whim. I didn't know why I'd even suggested it, except that I only had to think again of Juliana and her reaction to the feast for guilt to rear itself again.

I took a swig of my ale, wishing it were as easy to swallow the discomfort that arose whenever I thought about Juliana's dangerous situation. "What do you think, William? Should we give the peasants additional food? Ale? Perhaps for Michaelmas?" The feast of Saint Michael was only a week away, and would commence as the bulk of the harvesting was completed.

William took a step backward but bumped into a stool. "Such giving has never been done, my lord," he said, throwing out his arms to steady himself, but in the process one of his arms knocked against a stack of books on the shelf behind him, sending the volumes toppling to the floor.

I couldn't hold in a chuckle. William's clumsiness had always irritated my father, but the servant had been so meticulous with the ledgers and so wise with his financial counsel that Father had overlooked the man's faults.

"It's never been done, my lord," William repeated. "But with the growing tensions lately, a gift may help head off potential problems. It may indeed."

"Growing tensions?"

"It's nothing." Irene squinted at her needle as she re-threaded it. "Simply a stirring of discontent, likely produced by the Cloaked Bandit."

Cloaked Bandit. This time I stifled my laughter. If Irene knew she was afraid of a girl several years younger than her, she'd burn with mortification. "We have the means to give them gifts, do we not?" I directed my question to William.

"Plenty, my lord. As the numbers will attest." William leaned over the desk to point to a figure on the paper, but he knocked into several empty ink bottles.

"Then I appoint you to be in charge of arranging gifts, William." I folded the ledger closed, the matter settled. "Send them food, clothes, and the like. Whatever you think might be helpful."

Irene lowered her embroidery to her lap. "'Twould appear that no matter my counsel, you're determined to squander our father's fortune."

I stretched, past ready to move on to something more entertaining. "At least there's plenty to squander."

"I don't see anything humorous about the situation, Collin."

I'd noticed she wasn't calling me by my proper title. At first, her use of my given name had been something of a comfort, reminding me of the familial bonds I'd missed all the years I'd been gone. But for some reason, lately I'd sensed a note of condescension. Or maybe it had been there all along and I'd just been too happy to see her to notice.

My smile faded, and I sat forward. "I don't see any reason why you should care, Irene." I stressed her name. "You'll be married soon enough, and I'll make sure to send you to your new home with a handsome dowry."

She kept her focus on the needle pushing through the canvas. "I just don't want to see you deplete the family estate on foolish things, especially when I have worked so hard these past years to do as Father would have wanted."

"It's my estate now."

"Yes, you keep reminding me of that."

A knock on the door stopped the retort on the tip of my tongue. As William stumbled across the room to answer, I stared at Irene.

With her pale, unblemished skin and fair hair, she was a beautiful woman—regal, elegant, and every inch a lady. A large majority of our guests during the past month had been noblemen who were interested in winning Irene's hand in marriage. There had also been a fair share of young ladies and their parents who'd come to seek my favor.

I'd have to choose a wife from among the noblewomen eventually. Many of my friends were already married, including one of my closest friends and a fellow noble knight—Sir Derrick—who'd won the contest for Lady Rosemarie's love only that summer.

Now it was my turn. Especially after nearly falling in love with Lady Rosemarie myself, I was ready to find a woman just as kind and sweet and gentle. But first, I needed to locate a husband for Irene—and perhaps sooner rather than later.

"Lord Collin," William said as he turned from the open door. "One of your guests requests your presence."

Before I could reply, Juliana pushed past my steward into the study. I hadn't seen her yet that morning, as she'd been absent from the few guests who'd risen early enough to partake of a light fare of bread, fruit, and custards. I didn't imagine she'd overslept as many of the nobility were apt to do after staying up far into the night. And as I assessed her now, her eyes were bright, her cheeks flushed, and the hem of her gown wet with dew.

She'd been outside.

I didn't quite know what to think about that—whether to compliment her for looking pretty or to ask her if she'd been trying to get away.

"Lady Eleanora," I managed, rising from my chair.

Worried lines creased her forehead and she started to speak. But I slid my gaze toward Irene, and Juliana's followed suit. At the sight of my sister sitting near the hearth, the lines in her forehead quickly smoothed. "Lord Collin." She gave me the expected curtsey.

"I missed seeing you earlier this morning," I said lightly, only to realize how much I meant the words.

At my confession, Irene stopped mid-stitch and perused Juliana from her slippered toes to her curly hair, tied back with a silk ribbon that matched one of the gowns I'd had Mistress Higgins hang in the wardrobe—all chosen from the collection of Mother's garments Irene hadn't made over. The purple was the color of the amethyst gems sewn around the waist.

"You look lovely." The words slipped out before I could stop them.

Irene's attention jumped to me again and her eyes were filled with surprise.

I doubted she was surprised I'd given a beautiful lady a compliment. I was quite accomplished at flattery when I wanted to be.

But the sincerity? The awe in my voice? I astonished myself with how much the tone revealed.

However, Juliana didn't seem to hear me, and she didn't give Irene more than a passing glance as she crossed toward me.

"You'll be happy to know," I continued, "I was just in the process of planning gifts for the tenants on my land. Isn't that so, William?"

"Very true, sir." William stood awkwardly near the door.

Juliana quirked one brow, her expression more skeptical than approving. "I suppose that's a good first move for you, Lord Collin."

I smiled in satisfaction. "We have to start somewhere, don't we?"

"Yes, I suppose we do." But her voice wasn't convinced. She held out a folded piece of parchment. "Would you be so kind as to have one of your trusted servants deliver this missive to my family?"

I took hold of it, but she didn't immediately relinquish the letter.

"Due to the circumstances of my arrival, I have no doubt they will be worrying by now," she explained. "And I would like to prevent any trouble that might occur as a result."

From the serious set of her lips, I sensed she was concerned for her friends. They would surely be wondering what had become of her. "I'll have my swiftest—and most trusted—soldier deliver it right away."

"Thank you." She let go of the paper and took a step back, then glanced at Irene before leveling her gaze at me.

"I shall provide your trusted soldier with delivery instructions when he's ready to start."

I'd deliver the letter myself, but I didn't want Irene to know that. When I'd been out riding yesterday, I'd noticed that Juliana's young accomplice had come back to Goodrich land with another man. Even though they hadn't spotted me, I guessed they'd been searching for her. I'd have no trouble tracking them down if they were still on my land. They probably wouldn't let me get anywhere near them without riddling me full of arrows. So I'd have to sneak the letter into their camp and leave it anonymously.

"Perhaps you should invite your family." Irene spoke from behind us. "Lady Eleanora … What was it—Delacroix?"

Juliana's eyes flashed with a burst of anxiety that she rapidly smothered. "Yes, Delacroix." Her voice was cool and her expression again placid before she turned to face Irene. "Thank you for the kind offer to have my family visit. But I'm not staying long. I shall be returning home at week's end."

Irene studied Juliana's face. "I feel as though I've seen you before. But I'm certain that I've never had the privilege of meeting anyone from the Delacroix family."

Did Irene doubt the stories I'd spread about Juliana's arrival? I'd hoped the information I'd sparingly provided about her false past would silence gossipers. But apparently, Irene hadn't believed everything she'd heard. What if my sister recognized Juliana? Irene had indicated that she'd never had much contact with Charles Wessex and his daughter. From what I'd gathered since my arrival, our father's grudge had kept the two families apart since we were children. But if I'd remembered Juliana's beautiful hair after all of these years, what if Irene did too?

I tried to quell the wariness worming through my stomach and reminded myself that surely Irene would have no reason to suspect anything. Everyone believed Juliana Wessex had died along with her father.

Before I could think of an appropriate response, Juliana was answering calmly. "I'm sure you're simply confusing me with all of the other pretty ladies that Lord Collin has known."

"Perhaps. Nevertheless, you must stay longer. Don't you agree, Collin?"

"I agree completely. You'll break my heart if you leave too early."

"Oh, I'm sure your broken heart will mend quite easily," Juliana said, tossing a small smile at me.

"My lady," I said in mock surprise, returning her smile. "That's not true. You have *stolen* my heart. And when you leave, you shall take it with you."

At my reference to stealing, Juliana's smile moved to her eyes, turning them a warm brown.

"If you must leave so soon," Irene said, "then we shall have to do our best to entertain you while you're here with feasting, dances, and parties of every kind."

All traces of mirth vanished from Juliana's face. Before she could say something foolish to Irene—about extravagance or how much others were suffering—I spoke. "We're having an archery contest tomorrow."

Juliana's expression sparked with sudden interest.

"Collin is accomplished at the longbow as well as the crossbow," Irene added. "I'm sure you'll be quite impressed by his skill."

"Do you expect to win the contest?" Juliana asked me.

"No one has been able to beat him yet," Irene answered, tying a knot in her embroidery thread.

I had no reason to boast about my ability. For I doubted there was a nobleman in all the realm who would be able to defeat me. I'd worked for years to perfect my archery skill.

"If you're such the expert, my lord, then maybe I shall have to challenge you." The glint in Juliana's eye already challenged me.

Before I could answer, Irene gave a soft snort of condescension. "Such a display would be most unseemly, perhaps even scandalous."

I picked up the quill pen and twirled it, attempting to quell my eagerness to accept Juliana's challenge. "My sister is right."

"I think you're merely afraid of being defeated by a woman," Juliana said. "That would indeed be scandalous."

"Oh, I'm not afraid," I responded, unable to temper the arrogance in my voice. "Not in the least."

"Then if you don't mind a little unseemliness, I shall join your contest."

Irene protested again. But Juliana merely strode across the room and out the door without another word.

Even though I knew I ought to add my protest, I couldn't. The thought of an archery contest involving Juliana was too appealing to resist.

# Chapter
## 8

*"Perhaps Irene's judgment was correct."* Worry flashed across Collin's features as we strode toward the center of the field. "Perhaps you should sit with the ladies."

I fitted my bow over my shoulder and kept pace with his long steps. I had to carry the drawstring arrow bag since it certainly wouldn't look proper for me to don a belt and let it dangle at my waist as I was accustomed to doing. "I think you're just afraid I'll beat you."

The bright sunshine turned Collin's wind-tousled hair the color of warm butter. I tried not to look at his face, at his eyes that would be equally as warm—and disarming.

"I'm certain you're quite good," he said under his breath. "But after pondering the matter, that's why I don't think you should do this. Your skill may arouse suspicion."

I glanced to the tent where the other ladies were sitting. The canopy above them provided a cover from the sun, protecting their perfect complexions.

With my freckles and tanned skin, I was already different. Even if I had unblemished skin, I had absolutely nothing in common with the other ladies—not anymore. They flirted, and batted their eyes, and spoke of things that held no interest to me. I'd much rather participate in the archery contest with the men.

But Collin was right. I had to be careful to play the part of a noblewoman, though I detested it. I couldn't afford to draw attention to myself.

I stopped before reaching the men who'd gathered near the targets and were eyeing the brightly painted circles suspended from posts. My fingers twitched with the need to participate in the competition and show my skill, to show that I could shoot as well as any man.

"Maybe just a couple of shots?" I asked.

He hesitated. "You know I can't resist you. Not when you look at me like that."

"Look at you like what?"

"With your eyes so wide and pretty."

I felt an unbidden smile grow on my face.

He leaned closer and brushed a stray curl from my forehead.

"Lord Collin." One of his servants approached from behind. "I beg your pardon, my lord. This won't take but a moment." The young man slumped his shoulders and bent his head, as if waiting for a rebuke for interrupting. But instead of irritation, Collin clamped the man's arm in friendliness.

I took a step away and fidgeted with the hemp string and the nocking point on the bow while Collin conversed with his servant. His voice was kind as he patiently answered the servants' questions regarding details for the picnic they'd planned after the contest.

Maybe I could fault Collin for being a nobleman, but I couldn't find much else wrong with him. Since meeting him, he'd proven to be as good and kind as any of my friends back in the forest. I could honestly say I'd enjoyed his company yesterday when he'd taken me on a tour of his home, the stables, and some of the surrounding land. He'd regaled me with tales of his adventures during boyhood, as well as when he was a page with the duke. He'd made me laugh at his childhood antics and hold my breath at his dangerous deeds. And for just a little while, I'd forgotten about my other life and had been content simply being with him.

When the servant bowed and scurried away toward the shaded grove, where other servants were assembling the picnic, Collin returned to me.

"My lady." He held out his arm. His smile, his good manners, his sweetness—they were all endearing. Part of my mind rang out a warning that I ought to spurn him, to keep my distance, to push him away. But no matter how much I tried to dislike him, I couldn't. In fact, the longer I was with him, the harder it was to hold my childhood grudge. For today, at this moment, I merely wanted to enjoy the contest and perhaps forget again for a few moments that I was a hunted criminal.

With a return smile, I slipped my hand into the crook of his arm and allowed him to lead me toward the men.

Some of the contestants smirked when they noticed the bow and quiver full of arrows I was holding. I was tempted to slap their mirth away. But Collin joked with the men good-naturedly, and soon he convinced them to allow me to have a turn.

I waited at the end of the line, letting the fall sunshine caress my cheeks. I tried to not to dwell on the thought that while I was out in the open and free, somewhere not too far away my friends were still in hiding, with no life at all except to hunt, evade my uncle's men, and keep from getting caught.

Collin was the last of the men to shoot, and his arrow flew fast and hard, hitting the center of the target with a precision that was impressive. I didn't clap as the other ladies did, but when he turned and grinned at me I nodded my approval. "Well done, my lord."

"Nice of you to say so, my lady."

"Have your servant remove your arrow," I said as I took my position at the line. "And I shall bore mine into the same spot."

One of Collin's brows arched and was quickly accompanied by the laughter of several noblemen.

"Or at least I shall try," I amended, although it pained me to act more helpless than I was.

Collin bounded toward me. "If you're determined to match my shot, then you'll need a lesson or two from me." He winked at his friends, and then took position behind me. "Already I can see that you're holding the bow all wrong."

I could hear the men snickering, and my fingers tightened against the string. I'd show them. I'd let two arrows fly before they could blink.

Collin's steady hand wrapped around mine, stopping me. "Careful," he murmured against my ear. "Remember. You're Lady Eleanora Delacroix. Not the Cloaked Bandit."

His arm pressed against me, and he readjusted his fingers over mine so that he gave the appearance of helping me pull the string.

"I don't need a lesson." Even as I spoke the words, I couldn't keep from leaning back into him just slightly until I felt the gentle pressure of his chest.

"You might have more to learn from me than you think," he whispered. His voice near my ear and the warmth of his breath made my heart tumble like a pebble down a cliff.

"And perhaps you have something to learn from me too."

"I have no doubt I do." I could hear the smile in his voice. "In fact, I think my education began the moment I saw you."

At the teasing calls from several of the men, Collin tossed a flippant comment over his shoulder. "Don't rush me. She's quite the novice and has a great deal to learn."

His remark brought a chorus of guffaws from his friends.

"A novice?" I knew I ought to be insulted by his comment, but I couldn't think about anything except his hand upon mine and the gentle pressure of his arm. I was surrounded by him, and it was all I could do to focus on the target.

"In fact, I think I should like to give you archery lessons every day," he murmured, settling in closer.

I wanted to tell him I wouldn't object, but my breath had caught in my chest, and I couldn't speak past the tightness his nearness caused. His nose nuzzled in the hair above my ear, and then he dragged in a shaky breath. Was I affecting him the same way he was me?

"Come, Lord Collin," called a nobleman with a laugh. "Save the cuddling for the picnic. This is a serious contest."

Embarrassed heat slid around my middle. I pulled back on the string the rest of the way and then let go. At the same time, Collin leaned into my hair again and let out a large breath. Though my hair was thick, the heat from his exhalation soaked into me, taking me by surprise. I jumped and my bow swerved. The arrow flew forward with half the strength I normally exerted and barely hit the outer line of the target.

Collin released his hold, but didn't step away. "Looks like you'll need more target practice, my lady. And of course, I'm a willing teacher."

Amidst the chortles of his companions, Collin winked at me.

"Very well, my lord." I slipped another arrow out of the quiver standing next to me on the ground. Then with a mere glance, I notched, drew, and shot—this time with all my strength. "When would you like to give me another lesson?"

The arrow thumped into the target, and I knew I'd hit it dead center—hopefully in the same hole Collin had made. From the vanishing smiles of the noblemen and their gaping mouths, I guessed I'd come fairly close.

"What?" I asked with pretended innocence.

Collin gave me a slow grin. "'Twould appear you have amazing beginner's luck."

Only then did I glance at the target. My arrow protruded from a hole right next to the one Collin's had made. Frustration slithered through me. How had I missed?

Perhaps I'd allowed Collin's attention to distract me more than I'd realized.

"Or maybe I'm just a great teacher?" he asked, his eyes beseeching me to play along with him.

Denial sprang to my lips. But at the silence from the direction of the women's tent, I nibbled my bottom lip instead. They all wore stunned expressions—except Lady Irene. Her eyes had narrowed, and she stared at me with the same intensity as yesterday, when I'd spoken with her in the solar. She certainly suspected all was not as it seemed. Although I doubted she knew my true identity, since we hadn't seen each other since we were little girls, and then only in passing.

Once this past year, while hiding in a tree, I'd seen her riding with my cousin, Sir Edgar. I'd heard rumors that Sir Edgar was aspiring to win her hand. With such a large dowry, Uncle probably thought to gain even more with Edgar's union to Lady Irene.

Whatever the case, I knew I had to play my role as Lady Eleanora with as much authenticity as I could. I gave an inward sigh. "Don't praise your teaching skills too highly, Lord Collin," I said loud enough for the ladies to hear. "'Tis surely only beginner's luck."

My teasing drew the laughter of the men and titters from the women. Only Lady Irene remained unsmiling as though she saw past my charade. The survival instinct I'd honed over the years told me to flee—now, while I could. That if I waited, I'd only get into trouble.

But the soft touch of Collin's fingers upon my arm stopped me.

I turned to find his beautiful green eyes peering down at me with the usual humor I was coming to expect, along with something else, something that made my heart thump against my chest with a strange rhythm.

And suddenly, I realized I didn't want to leave. At least not quite yet.

# Chapter
# 9

A THOUSAND CANDLES LIT THE GARDEN, MAKING THE flower-filled crystal centerpieces sparkle. The small braziers placed among the tables were glowing red, providing heat for the guests who milled about the glittering party.

I'd wasted no expense on the garden dinner. The tables were spread with the richest of fare, and golden goblets along with the best silver I owned. I'd provided fur cloaks for my guests of the finest ermine and mink. I also had arranged for minstrels to play from a boat on the nearby pond among a hundred floating lanterns.

So far, it was my grandest party, even more elaborate than the one I'd planned for Lady Rosemarie when I'd been trying to win her heart. I surveyed the garden with a satisfied smile.

Maybe I hadn't been able to impress Juliana yet. But tonight's festivities would surely show her all she was missing with her self-imposed exile into the forest. And maybe, just maybe, I'd be able to convince her to give up her dangerous, thieving ways.

That's what I wanted, wasn't it?

I supposed from the moment I'd learned of her true identity, I'd decided she needed saving—saving from the reckless course of life she'd chosen. It was past time for her to take her rightful place again among the nobility and live the life to which she'd been born.

The fur trim of my velvet cloak brushed against my chin, reminding me of the softness of Juliana's hair. I told myself I wasn't attracted to her, that I hadn't gone to all the trouble of the party simply for her.

But when she finally stepped through the arched trellis into the spacious garden, my chest tightened with something akin to awe. Mistress Higgins had left Juliana's hair long and flowing, with a simple twist pulling it slightly back at her forehead. Though it was covered with a silky veil, I could still see it fell in curly waves down a striking black velvet cloak that highlighted the pale pink gown beneath.

How was it possible that every time I saw her, she grew more beautiful?

One of the noblemen next to me slapped my back with a laugh. "I suppose you'll be wanting to give her a few more lessons of a different kind this evening?"

I grinned, not caring that everyone saw me gawking at Juliana. I didn't mind if they believed I'd put my claim on her, because the truth was I didn't want to have to share her attention with anyone else.

I broke away from the teasing of the men and moved toward her. "There you are," I said, bowing before her. "You look more dazzling than all the candles, stars, and lanterns combined."

She gave me a shaky smile and smoothed her hand down the fluffy fur edge of her cloak. "This is too much, Collin."

"Not at all." I pulled a small box from my pocket and handed it to her. "For you."

"No more jewels."

I leaned toward her. "I can't help myself. Besides, I told you that whatever I give you, you get to keep at the week's end."

She took the box, hesitantly fingering the long, silky ribbon that held it closed. Then she gazed around the garden, her eyes growing wider as she took in the candelabras on each table, the mounds of delicacies, pastries, and countless other dishes. When her sights alighted upon the boat of minstrels, her brow creased and her lips pressed together.

"What do you think? Isn't it amazing?"

"You won't want to know what I really think." She pressed the box back toward me and started forward with choppy steps.

I reached for her arm so she couldn't escape. "You can tell me, sweetheart. I can handle the praise. I promise I won't let it go to my head."

She rolled her eyes. "I certainly won't be singing your praises, Lord Collin."

I pulled her to a halt away from the others so that we could talk without being heard. "I did all this for you. I thought you'd like it."

"If you thought I'd like this, then you don't know me at all."

A thin needle of hurt pricked me. "But . . ." I glanced around the lit garden. The glow from the fires and candles made it romantic. How could she not like it all?

She glared up at me.

"I'm sorry," I said, overcome with melancholy. After all the things she'd already said, I should have known she wouldn't like the display of wealth. Why hadn't I figured that out sooner? I could have planned something simpler.

"It seems like I just can't succeed when it comes to you. Everything I've done to earn your pleasure has been a complete failure so far."

She studied my face, and the lines in her forehead smoothed and her eyes softened. "Not a *complete* failure."

Something in her expression and tone sparked renewed hope inside me.

"I enjoyed praying with you in the chapel yesterday," she said, dropping her gaze almost as if her admission embarrassed her. "It's been a long time since I've been able to pray in a house of worship and partake of the Eucharist."

Although I prayed daily, I had to admit I'd relished the experience with her as well.

"And I enjoyed watching you receive your people today in the hall," she continued. "You listened carefully and dispensed justice and mercy wisely."

The hope rapidly fanned into a flame. Maybe I was proving I wasn't so despicable after all.

"I'm happy with simple things. But this ..." She lifted her head and waved at the tables and then toward the pond. "This is too much, Collin."

"So experiencing a taste of nobility doesn't make you wish you could return to this lifestyle?"

She shook her head slowly, sadly. "No. Never."

I sighed. "Then you're set on returning to your noble-thieving ways no matter what?"

"I'm afraid that even if I wished otherwise, I would have no choice."

I wanted to ask why. To finally get to the bottom of all that had happened in her past to drive her into the forest. But a group of people brushed near us and we lost our moment of privacy.

Juliana smiled sweetly and played the part of Lady Eleanora Delacroix to perfection. But throughout the evening, my mind kept turning over and over, attempting to find a way to make her change her mind about staying.

For some reason, I desperately hoped there was.

At the soft rap on my chamber door, I moved away from the window. Every night after I extinguished the lights—and after Mistress Higgins fell asleep on her pallet at the foot of my bed—I rose from the plush comfort of my bed, opened the window enough so that I could peer out into the forests that stood beyond the castle, and I reminded myself of my other life, of my friends who were out there sleeping on the hard earth, weary, cold, and hungry. Amidst the opulence, I didn't want to forget for a minute what their lives were like—and what my own would be like again in just two days.

The light knock came once more.

I hastened to the door before the sound could awaken Mistress Higgins. With my hand on the hunting knife I wore at all times, I cracked the door to reveal Collin.

"I finally figured out something you might enjoy," he whispered through a mischievous grin.

"Unless it involves a fair contest with bows and arrows, then I highly doubt I'll enjoy it," I countered, opening the door wider.

"Come with me." He reached for my hand.

"Like this?" I pulled back and glanced down at my nightdress.

He held out a heavy cloak with a fur-trimmed hood. "Cover up with this."

I hesitated. "I don't know if I should." It was surely past midnight.

"Don't tell me the Cloaked Bandit is scared," he teased.

I grabbed the cloak and tossed it around my shoulders. "Of course I'm not scared. I'm never scared."

"Never?" He grinned like a young page who'd gotten his way. "It's hard to believe you're *never* scared."

"Well, I'm not." I moved into the hallway ahead of him. The flickering light of his torch cast menacing shadows onto the stone walls of the deserted passage. I'd thrown out fear the day I'd found my father's remains in the gutter. I'd let anger drive out the fear, and I'd never allowed it to return.

"I count myself a brave man." Collin moved into place beside me and led the way. "But even brave people are afraid on occasion. Sometimes fear can protect us from being too foolish or reckless."

I didn't respond. I had the feeling Bulldog would agree with Collin. My friend had rebuked me many times for being reckless. But I wouldn't tell Collin that. Instead I allowed him to lead me up the spiraling stairway of one of the towers.

When we reached the end of the steps, I found myself climbing atop the highest turret of the castle. The cold night air greeted us. Pulling my cloak tighter, I rushed over to the crenellated wall and peered through one of the gaps over the dark expanse of world that spread out endlessly. The sliver of moon illuminated the landscape enough for my heart to swell with the splendor of the view.

I could feel Collin's presence next to me. "I imagine the view is especially spectacular in the daylight," I said in quiet awe.

"It is." He stared out at the land. And for a long moment, we were quiet together, squinting into the darkness at the various shapes of homes and barns beyond the village.

Finally, a gust of the frigid night air slapped against my cheeks and threatened to pull the hood from my head. I couldn't keep from shivering. Collin slid an arm around my waist and drew me into the crook of his arm, against the warmth of his solid frame and his fur cloak.

I didn't resist.

For several more minutes we stood without speaking, peering over the moonlit landscape. The millions of stars overhead spread out to the horizon. I released a long, contented breath and leaned against Collin. He tightened his hold, but didn't speak, almost as if the moment were too holy for words. A sense of peace stole over me. What *would* it be like to live this way? To stop fighting and to be at peace all the time? To have a husband? And maybe children someday?

I'd never considered the option of marriage. Not when I was a hunted fugitive.

But standing in Collin's strong embrace, I could almost believe that such an opportunity might eventually befall me. That maybe I'd find someone as kind as Collin.

Of course I'd never marry *him*.

I squirmed at the thought, my blood warming and surging into my face.

He loosened his hold and gently spun me around. "I thought you might like a midnight picnic." There, in the middle of the turret, spread on a thick bear skin, was a tray of fruit, cheese, and tarts along with steaming mugs of hot ale. A small brazier glowed red. And near the door stood Collin's steward, William, who had spilled something on his cloak and was now clumsily mopping at the spot.

"What do you think?" Collin asked, watching my face for my reaction.

I smiled. I could do nothing less. "It looks perfect."

He tugged me toward the picnic. "Good. I'm relieved you like it. If you didn't, I was going to have to throw myself off the tower to my utter destruction."

I laughed and allowed him to assist me to the ground. "I'm not completely hardened to the pleasures of life."

"Or the pleasure of my company?"

"You're tolerable."

"Only tolerable, my lady?" he asked, lowering himself next to me, laying on his side, and propping himself up on one elbow. His eyes twinkled with mirth.

"I suppose you'll not let me rest until I admit that I like your company?"

"You're getting to know me well."

The bantering was doing funny things to my stomach, but I was enjoying it too much to stop. "Very well, I'll admit. You're slightly more than tolerable."

He laughed. "I can see that you're quite adept at paying compliments."

"Yes, I'm available for flattery any time you need it." For a while we talked of little things, more about his experience living with the Duke of Rivenshire, of his closest friends Sir Derrick and Sir Bennet, of his recent years fighting battles on the country's borders.

I wasn't sure if it was the warmth of the conversation or of the ale that made a pleasant trail throughout my body, but I found myself comfortable and cozy, especially with the heat emanating from the small fire in the iron grill. Enough so that when Collin finally stopped talking and rolled over onto his back to stare up into the expanse of the sky, I couldn't resist the urge to brush a stray strand of his hair off his forehead.

Once I moved the lock, I pulled back, embarrassment flooding me.

But he scooted closer and laid his head in my lap. He situated himself, crossed his arms over his chest, and breathed out a deep sigh. "Ah, that's much better."

"So I'm to be your pillow, my lord?" I teased, my fingers twitching with the desire to comb his hair again. I glanced over at William, who sat just inside the tower door with a brazier of his own to warm himself. Although he wasn't directly watching us and couldn't hear our hushed conversation above the wind, I sensed his attention nonetheless.

"Yes. Of course." Collin resumed looking up into the sky, his eyes wide, his face relaxed. "Don't you know that's why I kidnapped you? I needed a pillow for my midnight picnics."

"Ah, the truth finally comes out." I tried to keep my insides from quivering with the pleasure at his nearness, but they did anyway. And as hard as I resisted, I finally lifted my fingers to his hair and touched another strand.

He closed his eyes and leaned into me.

I let my fingers comb his hair gently across his forehead. The silky strands sent shivers to my belly. "I suppose you turn all the ladies you capture into pillows."

"How'd you guess?"

How many ladies had he liked over the years? My hand stilled. "Do you make a practice of bringing all your lady guests up to the turret for midnight picnics?"

His eyes flew open and his gaze locked on mine with a swiftness and intensity that sent my heart pattering. "Are you jealous?"

"Absolutely not." I started to move away.

He grabbed my hands to keep me from leaving. "I can admit, you're the first lady I've ever brought here."

"I am?" I ceased struggling and only wished I could still my inward tumult as easily.

"You're also the first lady I've turned into a pillow."

The tense muscles in my back relaxed.

"Happy?"

I smiled. "Maybe."

"So now that I've confessed my abysmal love life to you, it's your turn to make confessions."

"What would you like me to confess?" I gave in to the desire to twist a thin piece of his hair between my finger and thumb.

"Have you ever been in love?" Even though the question was spoken in his lighthearted tone, his eyes turned suddenly serious.

I wanted to tease him in response, to attempt to make him jealous. But what good would that do? "I've never even thought about falling in love. How could I?"

He studied my face for a long moment. I warmed under his scrutiny. Did he think I was pathetic?

"Tell me what happened," he said softly. "Tell me everything."

He peered at me with such sincerity, somehow I knew I could trust him. I swallowed the bitterness that always rose whenever I thought about my past. And then I told him. Everything.

I told him about the day my uncle—my father's stepbrother— had ridden into Wessex Castle with his son and his small army. How we'd believed he'd come in peace, until he'd entered the gates and surrounded us, forcing us to leave without anything but the clothes upon our backs. He'd promised to let Father live, as long as he took a new identity and didn't cause any trouble. At the time, I hadn't known that my uncle used me as his bargaining tool, had threatened to take me away from my father if he didn't do what my uncle asked of him.

For many years, my father and I lived in a remote village in obscurity, letting the rumors of his death circulate unchallenged. He'd lived as a peasant and worked as a blacksmith. As a young girl of only ten, I'd adjusted to my new life without difficulty and had even grown to love the people in our new village. I'd thought my father had been happy too.

Little had I known, all those years he'd secretly been planning an uprising, especially when Uncle's greed caused him to seek more wealth. Uncle had raised the taxes until the suffering grew unbearable. He'd taken away the homes and livelihoods of those who couldn't meet his increasing demands. And in their hungry desperation, many had started hunting on forbidden ground.

Uncle's laws tightened and the people's suffering increased. The desire for revolt swelled. As the rightful heir to Wessex, my father, had always treated his people kindly. He promised that if they helped restore him to his place of leadership, he'd do all he could to help ease their suffering.

The rebellion lasted for weeks. But in the end, Uncle's well-trained and well-armed soldiers overpowered the rebels. My father had been mortally wounded and had lain bleeding to death upon the dirt floor of our thatched peasant home. By then I'd been almost a woman, a young girl of fifteen. My father's best friend and fiercest warrior, Bulldog, had finally tied me up and dragged me from my father's side kicking and screaming.

If I'd stayed any longer, Uncle's men would have captured me too. My fate would have been the same as Father's—cruel torture and death. Instead, Bulldog had promised Father he would take me to safety and protect me. Rumors were spread from town to town that I had died of illness shortly before my father's capture, and we'd prayed the deception would work. Bulldog had even created a false grave, in case my uncle should require some sort of evidence.

"I've been living in the forests ever since," I finished. My shoulders slumped and my head bent, the defeat of the past weighing heavily upon me.

"So that means you've been living in the forests for two— almost three—years?" His voice was hoarse, and his face lined with fierce anger.

I nodded. "But I've survived. Bulldog taught me everything he knew. And now I'm stronger than most men."

"And you've had to steal to survive." He spat the words bitterly.

My loose hair fell over my shoulders and covered my face, hiding my shame. There were times, like this, when I knew my father wouldn't have been proud of the thief I'd become. Through all his trials and difficulties, he'd never resorted to thieving or breaking the law. He'd always insisted upon doing things the right way, in a way that pleased God.

But look where his noble ways had gotten him.

I tried to conjure the usual anger, to make myself hate my uncle and Edgar. But for some reason, with the heavens open above me, I couldn't summon the usual bitterness. I only felt empty. And sad.

With a sigh, I shifted away from Collin. But before I could extricate myself, he reached for my face and cupped his hands on my cheeks, forcing me to look down at him.

"You've been gravely wronged by your father's brother." His eyes were hard. "Let me help you fight against your uncle and restore what's rightfully yours."

I shook my head. Nightmares still haunted me, nightmares of my father's mutilated body, along with the horrors I'd seen soon after. Uncle hadn't with stopped at torturing my father— he'd also made a spectacle of burning to death all the other peasants he'd captured, all the brave people who'd participated in the uprising. I'd watched with Bulldog and Thatch from the confines of the forest, inwardly screaming as the agonized cries of so many friends and neighbors rose into the air. How could I bear to witness such a cruelty ever again?

"It's safer this way," I said in a low voice. "My friends and I will be fine as long as my uncle believes I'm dead."

Collin shook his head. "We can fight him."

"No."

"I can raise a large army. I can even call upon the Duke of Rivenshire."

I started to pull away from Collin again, but he only drew my head down toward his so that my face was mere inches away. My hair hung like a curtain around us, shielding our faces but still allowing light from the brazier to glow upon us.

His hand slid to the back of my neck, digging deeply into my hair. His gaze dropped to my lips. And his breath grew ragged and brushed against me.

Suddenly thoughts about my past, all the pains and frustrations, disappeared. All I could think about was how close I was to Collin, how I could lower my face the merest fraction and feel his warm breath even more.

I liked the intense hold he had on the back of my neck. I liked the way his fingers had splayed on my cheeks, caressing my skin. And I couldn't keep from studying his lips, slightly parted—almost as if he was planning on kissing me.

The smallest amount of pressure of his hand on my neck bent me closer so that my lips had no choice but to brush against his. At the brief contact, a popping erupted in my belly, like dry wood in a firepit. When he lifted his head from my lap and pressed his lips against mine with more urgency, I was helpless but to respond. I let my lips move against his for an endless second.

At a clearing throat near the turret doorway, I gasped and sat back, breaking the connection with Collin. I scrambled to my knees, heat spilling through me in a confusing disarray.

Collin too hastened to put distance between us. He climbed to his feet and jammed his fingers into his hair—almost as if he were frustrated with himself. "I'm sorry."

I rose to my feet, my chest heaving as I worked to catch my breath.

"I didn't mean for that to happen." He cocked his head toward his steward by the door. "That's exactly why I'd asked my most trusted servant to stay. To act as a chaperone."

I couldn't bear to look at the servant. I'd never kissed a man before. Never even thought about it. How had I lost all reason now? With Collin?

Collin nodded at the older man. "Thank you, William."

The servant cleared his throat again. "Just doing what you asked me to, my lord."

"I guess this will be our one and only midnight picnic," Collin said with a shaky laugh. "I'm apparently not quite as self-controlled as I thought I would be."

I nodded, growing more embarrassed by the second, and started toward the door. But I only made it a step before he grabbed my hand and halted me.

"Do you forgive me?" His face was haggard and his eyes pleaded with me.

"There's nothing to forgive, Collin," I said, forcing lightness into my tone. I didn't want him to see how much his kiss had affected me, how much I'd liked it. "We were caught up in the emotion of the moment. That's all. Let's not make anything more of it. It meant nothing."

He studied my face. "Very well." Disappointment edged his voice.

I slipped my hand out of his and continued toward the doorway, unable to meet the gaze of the servant standing there. And I was unwilling to let Collin see my face again for fear he would know that the kiss *was* something. Something very special. It meant much more than I could ever acknowledge.

# Chapter 10

*I was losing the challenge.*

I fingered the bulges in the velvet bag, the hard ridges of the gold coins. Then I trailed my fingers over the diamond necklace, against the smooth, glittering stones.

Only one day left, and I would be able to take the gold and the jewels and leave.

With a curt shake of my head, I pushed in the small drawer of the wardrobe, shutting the riches out of sight.

The night I'd arrived at the castle, I truly had believed I'd never stop loathing Collin. But after his kiss the previous evening, I couldn't deny the truth any longer. I liked Collin Goodrich. In fact, I liked him very much—so much that every time I thought about the midnight picnic and the warmth of his lips against mine, I wanted to swoon. And I was certainly not the swooning kind of girl.

It wasn't just the kiss that had me second-guessing myself. It was everything about the time with him: how he'd tried so hard to please me, to find something I'd enjoy; how we'd been able to talk openly; how I'd finally been able to bare my soul to someone, to share the deep pains of my past. He'd listened and understood me, and he'd even been angry over the injustices I'd suffered.

"William is here to escort you to the ball, my lady," Mistress Higgins said behind me.

I straightened and smoothed the skirt of the loveliest gown I'd donned yet. When Mistress Higgins had held up the mirror after assisting me and fixing my hair, I almost had refused to look. But I'd finally given in to the need to see myself. I'd told myself only to scoff. But at the reflection of an elegant lady, I'd stared in amazement. I hadn't recognized myself in the dark, rich plum gown. Maybe for tonight—just tonight—I'd allow myself to forget about reality. Maybe I'd pretend that this was my life, that Father was still alive, and that Uncle had never come.

"Are you ready, my lady?" Mistress Higgins asked again, gently tucking one of my stray curls up into the high, elegant knot at the back of my head.

"You're a dear woman." I squeezed the woman's gnarled hand. "You've been much too kind to me."

"It's been my pleasure to serve you, my lady." Mistress Higgins smiled, her eyes crinkling at the corners of her perpetually wrinkled face. "Since your arrival, Lord Collin has finally been happy. You're apparently just what he needed."

"Oh, I doubt that." If only Mistress Higgins knew who I really was.

As I accepted William's arm, his eyes widened behind his eyeglasses. Although his expression gave nothing away, I couldn't keep from wondering how much he'd overheard of my conversation with Collin the previous evening on the tower. He'd been a fair distance away. And Collin had claimed the man was his most trusted servant.

Nevertheless, I should have used more caution in sharing so much about my past in his presence.

"My lady," William said kindly, tripping over his feet as we started down the passageway that led to the Great Hall. "You look lovely this evening."

"Thank you, William. Much better than when I arrived, no doubt."

He stumbled again. And I could only pray he was truly as dependable as Collin said.

I glided along, the soft strands of music from the ball already wafting into the far regions of the castle. I found myself anticipating the dance. Even though it had been years since I'd attended an event such as this, I was sure my feet would easily fall into the rhythm of the many dance steps I'd learned in the past.

When I arrived at the doorway of the Great Hall, my heart swelled with the music and my eyes feasted upon the couples who were already swirling. The trestle tables had been pushed against the walls to make more room for the guests. The rush mats had been strewn with fresh herbs, which now rose to perfume the air under the crushing feet of the dancers. And the wall sconces and large hearth fire lit the room, making the jewels that studded the garments of the noblemen and ladies sparkle.

As if he'd been watching for my appearance, Collin stopped mid-sentence while conversing with a group of guests, including Lady Irene. He excused himself and crossed toward me, his face alight with admiration.

"I've been waiting to see you," he said when he stood before me. His gaze caressed my cheeks, my nose, and then my lips.

Heat flared in my stomach. Was he remembering our moment in the tower?

When his eyes lifted to mine, the hue was dark, almost pine green. Everything within the depths proclaimed his memory of our kiss and his wish to do so again.

I pressed my hand against the satiny fabric at my stomach, warding off the strange fluttering. "You only saw me two hours ago. Surely you aren't anxious to see me again so soon." We'd spent most of the afternoon dividing up the goods William had purchased to give to the neediest families within the Goodrich lands. Collin had suggested making bundles and packaging one for each family, consisting of food, blankets, wool cloth for sewing into garments, and an assortment of other items. At first, I'd suspected Collin was suggesting the charity to impress me. But as the afternoon progressed, I could sense a genuine desire in him to understand what my life as a peasant was like and to help those less fortunate.

"Every minute away from you is too long," he said. "But it's been worth the wait, because you're the most beautiful woman here."

"You say that every time I see you," I teased, hoping to lighten the moment and make us both forget about the attraction that was growing with each passing day.

"I only ever tell the truth, my lady."

I was relieved when he grinned and held out his arm.

"Ah, Lady Eleanora." Lady Irene crossed toward us. "You look very nice this evening. Purple is a becoming color on you. It goes so well with your red hair."

Something in the way Lady Irene said the word *red* made me flinch inwardly. Was she mocking my hair color as Collin had childishly done so long ago? Or was there something more going on?

"You look very nice this evening too, Lady Irene." I eyed her silky blue gown. "'Twould appear that blue is a good color for you, since it goes so well with your *yellow* hair."

Lady Irene's brow shot up at the comment. She hadn't been overly friendly with me that week. She'd clearly not approved of the gift bundles Collin was orchestrating, and I suspected she thought I was encouraging him in the endeavor—which, indirectly, I was.

But I only smiled with what I hoped conveyed innocence.

Collin chuckled. "I must warn you, Irene. Never say anything about Lady Eleanora's hair color, unless you wish to find yourself with a new enemy."

Lady Irene managed a strained half smile. "Since you're finally here, Lady Eleanora, why don't I take you around and introduce you to some of our newly arrived guests." She slipped her arm into mine as if we were sisters and tugged me away from Collin.

As we stepped forward, the crowd parted—and that was when I saw them. I froze, suddenly paralyzed. My heart stopped. And my breath caught.

There, only a dozen feet away, stood a tall, older man without one strand of gray in his raven-black hair. His noble face was pockmarked, almost scaly—ravaged from a childhood illness. And he was attired in the pristine white tunic and breeches he'd always worn.

It was none other than my uncle.

Standing next to him was Edgar, his face a much more handsome version of Uncle's. He was laughing at something one of his companions said, but when his gaze alighted upon Lady Irene, his smile smoothed into one more calculated and clever.

I wrenched away from Lady Irene and spun. My heartbeat slapped against my ribs like the rapid flapping of hawk wings. I had to get away. Now. Before they recognized me.

"Lady Eleanora?" Lady Irene reached for my arm. "Whatever is the matter? Are you ill?"

I couldn't respond. Bile swirled in my stomach, and for an instant I thought I'd be able to honestly answer Lady Irene that, yes, I was indeed going to be sick to my stomach.

At the sight of my face, Collin's mouth creased into a frown. When he peered in the direction of Uncle and Edgar, his brow dropped into a sharp scowl. He grabbed my arm and began to steer me toward the door.

Lady Irene hastened after us. "Lady Eleanora, you look like you've seen a ghost."

"I told you not to invite George Wessex and his son," Collin shot at his sister over his shoulder. "In fact, if I remember correctly, I strictly forbade it."

I stumbled next to Collin, my pulse pounding with the frantic need to escape from the room before Edgar or my uncle spotted me. I wasn't afraid, was I? Hadn't I told Collin I never feared anything?

But dressed as a woman, attired in finery and with only my hunting knife buried beneath my skirt, a reminiscent twinge of panic rushed through me—the same kind of fear I'd had that day so long ago, when Uncle had ridden into the inner bailey of Wessex Castle, unsheathed his sword, and ordered my father to leave.

Irene followed us out the door and into the hallway. "I don't understand why you're suddenly opposed to having Lord Wessex and his son attend our parties. Haven't I made it quite clear to you that I favor Edgar for a match? That he's one of the few noblemen who presents a worthy option for my dowry?"

"You disobeyed me, Irene." Collin's voice was sharp and his face taut with anger. "I told you not to invite them, and you did so anyway."

"I didn't think it would make any difference," Irene offered in a placating tone, as if she realized she'd pushed her brother too far. "I didn't know their presence would disturb Lady Eleanora so much. In fact, I didn't realize she even knew them."

"You don't have to understand everything. But I still expect that while you live in my home, you'll follow my instructions."

Lady Irene's eyes narrowed. "Edgar is almost my betrothed."

"Not anymore."

"You cannot decide for me—"

"I have every right to decide." Collin's voice was low and threatening. "It's my job to protect you."

Lady Irene lifted her chin.

Collin turned to me and his features softened. "Will you be all right?"

I took a deep breath and tried desperately to bring myself under control. "I shall be well enough once I have a breath of air." All I wanted to do was get away from the Great Hall, away from Lord Wessex and Sir Edgar and any chances that they might recognize me.

The rational part of me knew I had nothing to worry about. It had been years since they'd seen me. Nevertheless, I felt oddly bare. My fingers clenched with the need for my bow and arrows. After the cruelty I'd witnessed from my uncle and cousin, I wouldn't dare stand in the same room as them without the means to protect myself.

❧

I WAS TEMPTED TO TELL MY GUARDS TO ESCORT GEORGE Wessex and his son off my land. I sorely wanted to tell the black-hearted thieves to leave and never come back—after I gave them both the beating they deserved.

But I couldn't do so without arousing suspicion. Already, Juliana's strange behavior and subsequent absence had caused enough gossip among the guests. I'd forced myself to stay through dinner and several dances so that I wouldn't bring further attention to her. Even though my muscles had ached with the need to grab Lord Wessex around the throat every time the man had spoken, I'd feigned politeness.

Like the other guests, Lord Wessex had inquired after "Lady Eleanora." But thankfully he'd rapidly lost interest in her, and instead had focused all of his attention on Irene and

Edgar. He kept laying hints about how much they liked one another and what a lovely match they'd make. I wanted to tell him I'd never in this lifetime or the next give Edgar permission to marry Irene. But I decided that I'd save that conversation for another evening.

After I'd stayed as long as I could possibly endure, I'd slipped out the back door of the Great Hall.

"Collin, wait." Irene rushed after me with a soundless tread.

I stopped, trying to squelch my irritation. "Yes?"

Her cheeks were flushed a pretty color of pink. She truly looked lovely that evening. I knew I should compliment her and reassure her about her future, as she was clearly worried about it. Since I'd been home, I hadn't taken the time to look after her well-being as I should. Silently, I promised myself that I would once matters were settled with Juliana.

She looked up with the vulnerable, sweet eyes of the girl I'd known so long ago. "Please, won't you at least speak with Lord Wessex about a potential match?"

"Absolutely not." The words were out before I could temper my emotion. "I give you my word that I shall find a suitable match for you soon. But I won't consider any union with that snake."

The sweetness vanished from her expression, replaced by hard, chiseled anger. "I don't understand why you're so against him. You hardly know him."

"I know what Wessex did to his brother and niece."

"His brother was senile. And he wasn't the rightful heir anyway."

"Those are just lies."

"And how would you know?"

I bit back a rush of words that surely would have given away Juliana. As much as I longed to defend the rightful heir to Wessex, I knew I had to pretend to be more ignorant than

I was. "It doesn't matter, Irene. I've already told you once, I won't consider a union with Edgar Wessex. Please resign yourself to my decision."

She stiffened and clenched her fists at her side. "How dare you come home after all this time and think you know what's best for me. Perhaps you can sweep into Goodrich and take away all of the finances and ruin Father's fortune with your carelessness. But you can't ruin my life too. I won't let you."

I sighed with frustration. I didn't have time right now to have this conversation. I was too anxious to see how Juliana was faring. "I'm sorry, Irene. You may not understand my decision now, but someday you'll thank me." I turned away from her and started up the spiraling steps of the tower that led to the upper floors of the castle.

"I won't thank you, Collin," she called after me. "I wish you'd never come home."

I blocked out Irene's frustrated comment as I raced up the stairway. The dark shadows of the passageway taunted me. The coolness of the night air blew in through the narrow arrow slits positioned in the tower walls.

What had I been thinking to invite Juliana to stay at my castle? Had I really believed she'd be able to hide her identity from everyone? Had I only put her in more danger?

My gut tightened.

Upon hearing Juliana's story the previous evening, I'd had thoughts of rallying my small army and charging over to Wessex right away, storming the castle and enacting justice. But after a sleepless night, I'd instead written a missive to the Duke of Rivenshire and sent it with one of my fastest riders. Surely my wise advisor would be able to give me direction on how to proceed. Once I heard back from him and had assurance of his help, perhaps then I could reveal everything to Irene. Until that point, I'd have to live with her anger.

I was breathing heavily by the time I reached the door that led to Juliana's chamber. I sucked in a breath in an attempt to calm my racing pulse, and then I rapped on the door.

After a long moment of silence, I knocked again, this time louder.

Still, there was no answer.

I cocked my ear, straining to hear, praying Juliana was merely asleep.

"Juliana?" I cracked the door open and peeked in. The dim light of the sconces revealed an empty room. Mistress Higgins, assuming she would have the evening free, was likely dining on leftovers with the other servants in the kitchen.

But where was Juliana?

I pushed the door wider and stepped in. I scoured the room until my gaze alighted upon a purple gown discarded upon the floor in front of the open doors of the wardrobe.

How had she changed out of the tight garment without the help of her lady's maid?

I crossed the room and lifted the gown, noting the sharp cuts in the bodice where she'd obviously hastily freed herself of the confines. A quick assessment of the wardrobe showed all the other gowns left untouched. I shoved them aside to search for her original breeches and tunic, which I'd instructed Mistress Higgins to stow in a back corner.

My fingers probed along the rear walls and then the entire length of the floor.

There was no trace of her garments.

Moving quickly, I jerked open the drawer at the bottom of the wardrobe where she'd stored the gold pouch and jewelry I'd promised her.

The red pouch peered back at me, and the diamond necklace winked.

My shoulders sagged, and I released the breath I hadn't realized I'd been holding. She wouldn't have left without taking the gold and jewels. Would she?

A breeze sifted through the open window, bumping the wooden shutter against the stone wall so that it clattered. Maybe she'd just gone outside to walk in the castle gardens, to get the breath of fresh air as she'd wanted.

I wished I could believe that.

I jumped up and ran to the window. The blackness of the moonless night met me. The clouds hung low and a drizzle had begun to fall. It would be the perfect night to escape, I admitted. No one would suspect that she'd leave under such conditions.

I returned to the bed and glanced underneath to the spot where she'd stored her bow and arrows. They were gone.

I expelled a sigh of frustration. I had no doubt now that she'd made her escape while everyone was busy at the ball and while the servants were occupied with their feast. If she were stealthy enough, she'd likely been able to escape without any detection, even from the guards standing watch at the gatehouse.

I glanced again at the open drawer, at the bag of gold. But why hadn't she taken the pouch or the necklace? I'd witnessed the way her eyes had lit the first time I'd shown her the gold. She'd wanted it. Desperately. Enough that she'd stayed, in spite of her clear desire to bolt the first chance she could.

Even as I asked the question, I knew the answer. Her honor wouldn't let her take them since she'd failed to complete our bargain, although she'd only been one day short.

Tomorrow was to have been our last day here at the castle, and I'd planned to have her help me deliver all of the bundles we'd packaged. After spending hours with her that week, I'd finally realized what would make her happy. And I'd wanted to end our time here by showing her that I wasn't such a dolt after all.

Sure, maybe I'd started off planning to give the packages for her sake. Every time I thought about her being out in the world cold, hungry, and clothed in rags, I wanted to do something to help others in the same situation. But the longer I'd worked with William on the project, the more I'd wanted to do this because it felt right. If God had blessed me with much, the least I could do was bless others in return.

I wiped a hand across my eyes and fought off sudden weariness. And, yes, disappointment.

The glint of something came from the center of her bed, among folds of the coverlet. I stretched out my hand and my fingers connected with a circular band.

My ring.

I straightened and held it up into the candlelight.

Diamonds in the shape of a cross gleamed within the silver setting. It was the ring I'd worn since receiving my knighthood from the duke, the one I'd tossed to her that morning when she'd robbed me.

I'd made sure when I kidnapped her that I left the bag of stolen goods for her waif of a companion. I'd wanted the boy to have something to take with him. She'd obviously kept my ring apart from the other items. But why?

My mind spun back to last night when I'd pulled her face down to mine, when I'd taken her smooth cheeks into my hands and captured her lips against mine. The heat the memory elicited wrapped around my middle.

She hadn't resisted my kiss, hadn't pulled away from me in shock or disgust. In fact, she'd met my kiss with a warm fervor that had surprised me. For all her resistance to my nobility and her insinuation that she would never like me, maybe she had a soft spot for me after all.

I twisted the ring around, and a grin tugged at my lips. Under any other circumstances, I would have let it loose into a full smile.

But the grin all too quickly fell away as the truth of the situation hit me.

What had started as a fun, flirtatious week to distract me from my melancholy had turned into something much more. I'd begun to care deeply about Juliana Wessex. As a neighbor. As a friend. And even as a woman. Now that she'd run out of my life, I realized just how much I didn't want to lose her. And how frightened I was that something would happen to her.

With a groan, I rose to my feet. The thought of her returning to her thieving ways and of getting caught scared me to the very core of my being. Certainly, it was only a matter of time before she was arrested for her petty thefts. They'd chop off her hand.

Or worse . . .What if she was captured and taken to Lord Wessex? What if he realized the Cloaked Bandit was really a woman?

My blood ran cold at the thought of what Lord Wessex might do to her, of the torturous ways he'd violate her. He'd make a spectacle of her, regardless of whether he ever discovered she was his long-lost niece.

"Blessed Mary," I whispered. I had to find her and stop her from stealing again. I had to bring her back and keep her safe.

I grabbed the pouch of gold and the jewels she'd left behind. And then I slipped the ring back on my finger.

It was past time for her to settle down and live like a lady. I just prayed I'd be able to convince her of the same.

# Chapter
## 11

I KNELT AND BRUSHED ASIDE FALLEN LEAVES TO REVEAL A footprint in the mud. Narrowing my eyes, I studied the forested area as I had a hundred times in the last hour. What clues had I missed?

I sat back on my heels, and the hairs on the back of my neck rose again.

Someone was following me. Or watching me. Or both.

I'd sensed the presence several hours ago, but so far whoever it was had kept well hidden.

And so had Juliana.

I'd started tracking her at first light. Of course I'd longed to leave as soon as I'd discovered that she'd gone. But I hadn't wanted to cause any more suspicion than necessary. So I'd stayed through the end of the dance, even though every second had been torture, especially each time I glanced toward Lord Wessex and his son. Irene had been angry with me all evening as well, and had made a point of spending much of the night with Edgar.

If only she knew the truth about our neighbors and what they'd done to Juliana and her father.

At the almost silent crack of a twig, I straightened and flattened my back against a large oak. The mist and the rain-drenched forest had dampened my garments hours ago, and now they stuck to my frozen limbs.

I'd easily tracked her into the thick Wessex forest. I'd even managed to keep her trail for several hours, traveling deeper into the heart of the woods. But somehow, somewhere, she'd disappeared. Her trail had just vanished. And no amount of searching had revealed any further hints of where she'd gone.

At first I'd been afraid that the worst had happened—that she'd been captured. But after calming my crazy heartbeat, I'd realized the vegetation showed no signs of struggle. There were no broken branches, no crushed leaves, no hoofprints, no twisted limbs. Nothing.

And that was my problem. I'd reached a dead end.

I stifled a frustrated sigh. If only I'd left right away. I would have caught up with her in no time, and we'd be back at the castle where I could talk sense into her.

But now . . .

I swallowed the constriction that held my lungs captive. I wasn't accustomed to panic. I was always in control, had always maintained the upper hand against my enemies.

But I was most definitely starting to panic at the thought of losing Juliana.

I surveyed the treetops. Hidden in the thick spruce, I located at least one peasant with an arrow pointed at my heart. Should I give myself up to the man? Or should I fight?

If I killed the peasant, I risked losing a potential link that might lead me to Juliana. But if I allowed myself to be captured, there was the chance I could discover more about where Juliana had gone. But only if the man was part of Juliana's band of followers. And even if he was, I had no guarantee that he'd be willing to take me to her, that he wouldn't attempt to rob and kill me first. Even if I wasn't Lord Wessex or Sir Edgar, my nobility still made me an enemy.

My muscles tightened with the need to fight, to fit an arrow into my bow and shoot the peasant out of the tree before he knew what hit him. But I pushed down my pride and slowly stepped away from the tree, bracing myself for the impact of the man's arrow.

It came swiftly. Instead of puncturing my body, it sliced through the loose fabric in the arm of my cloak, pinning it to the tree. Another arrow followed, pinning the other arm as well. A third arrow grazed the hood of my cloak and embedded into the tree with a twang.

"Don't move," came a growling voice, "or I'll make sure the next arrow hits your foot."

My knightly instincts and training demanded that I free myself from the arrows and defend myself. But I couldn't do anything foolish. Or I'd lose the chance of finding Juliana.

Within seconds, a short but stocky peasant was at my side, pressing a knife against my throat. He was outfitted in a greenish-gray cloak that blended in well with the woodland. "Who are you and why are you here?"

If I admitted the truth, would the man slice my throat open at once?

"And don't tell me you're hunting, or I'll cut out your heart and eat it for lunch." The man's grip was tight in spite of missing thumbs.

"I'm looking for someone," I said. "I thought maybe you could help me."

"The only help you'll get from me is a knock in the head and a boot out of the forest."

I stretched away from the blade, glad it was dull. "She left something behind. And I want to deliver it to her."

Beneath the coarse linen of the hooded cloak, fierce, dark eyes peered at me from within a fleshy face that was weathered and streaked with grime.

"It's a pouch I think she'll want," I continued.

Before I had the time to react, the man swung one of his stocky arms and plunged his fist into my stomach. The force knocked the wind from me and would have doubled me over had I not been pinned to the tree by arrows.

"Give me the pouch," the man barked.

"I have to deliver it to her personally."

The man smashed his fist into my gut once again.

Pain ricocheted from my stomach to my ribs, and I couldn't hold back a grunt. I clenched my fingers together to stop myself from lashing back. Instead, I allowed the peasant to smash me again, this time in the cheek. My head whacked into the hardwood with enough force that I had to blink away dizziness. He fumbled at my cloak, feeling for the hard lump that would alert him to the treasure I'd brought. But after a moment of patting me down, he was still empty-handed.

"Give me the pouch now. Or I'll kill you." The man's lips pulled back into a growl that revealed his teeth, and his short fingers slid around my throat. But even though the man was dangerous, I'd been around enough criminals during my lifetime to know that this man was no killer. He might hurt me, but I didn't think he would really kill me.

"Take me to Juliana and then I'll give you everything," I choked out through my constricting throat.

"I'll kill you before I ever take you to her." The fingers pressed at just the right spot to cut off my air. Ah, so he did know Juliana and where she was hiding. My sacrifice was paying off—if he didn't kill me first.

I wanted to struggle to catch my next breath. But I didn't move. Instead, I met the man's gaze. There in the depths of the sharp, dark eyes was exactly what I'd hoped to see, an intense protectiveness for Juliana.

As blackness slid through my consciousness, I prayed the peasant would see the same thing reflected in my own.

Pain radiated in my head, and I fought through the darkness to regain my wits. My fingers twitched against straw and the cold earth.

Where was I?

Voices penetrated the fog clouding my mind. I was tempted to open my eyes. Instead, I kept myself motionless and listened.

"You didn't need to hurt him," came a woman's voice.

"You're lucky I didn't kill him," answered another.

"I told you to be gentle."

"I was."

My chest expanded with sudden and overwhelming relief. I'd found her.

I lifted my lashes only slightly so that I caught a glimpse of Juliana standing several feet away in what appeared to be a dirt cave of some kind.

She stood before the same short, stocky man who had battered me, her hands pressed into her hips and her eyes narrowed in a glare. The man stared back with a scowl that would have made most girls cry.

When the sturdy peasant glanced in my direction, I let my lashes fall and feigned unconsciousness.

"I don't trust him," the man snarled in a low voice.

"Well, I do," came Juliana's quick, clear answer.

Inwardly, I smiled. Maybe I'd made more progress with her during our time together than I'd realized.

"I think he was being followed," the man said. "He could lead us into a trap."

I wanted to sit up in protest, but thankfully Juliana beat him to it. "Collin wouldn't try to trap me."

"He's a nobleman"—the peasant spat the words—"and the only good nobleman is a dead one."

For a long moment the cave was quiet, except for the crackling of wood in a fire across from me. I was close enough that I could feel the warmth of the flames, but far enough away that the dark shadows provided some privacy.

I peeked from between my lashes again and this time saw the young, thin accomplice who had ridden with Juliana the day she'd robbed me. Beyond the boy stood several other peasants, their shoulders stooped and heads bent under the low roof of the cave. Strangely, strands of what appeared to be roots hung from the ceiling. The light from several torches illuminated the crumbling dirt walls and a nearby tunnel.

I closed my eyes and breathed in the mustiness of damp earth that mingled with wood smoke. I dug through the straw until my fingers brushed against the soil of the floor. It was hard, almost clay-like.

Were we underground?

"Collin Goodrich might be a nobleman," Juliana finally said, "but he's kind."

"And kidnapping you was kind?" the man retorted.

If the peasants made their homes in underground caves, that would explain why I'd lost track of her. She'd likely entered through some secret passageway they'd made impossible to locate.

"I don't care what you think about Collin," Juliana said. She was attired in men's garments, and she'd tucked her hair up into her knit cap. Even so, now that I knew she was a woman, I didn't understand how anyone could miss seeing her for the beautiful lady she was.

"I've had the chance to get to know him," she said, "and I like him."

I had to stifle another smile. She liked me. Suddenly the battering and humiliation I'd taken at the hands of the growling peasant was worth it.

The gruff man grumbled again. "If you don't want me to kill him, then I say we dump his body back on Goodrich land."

"But he's hurt," she protested. "I think you broke a couple ribs and gave him a concussion." Her voice drew nearer.

I forced myself into absolute stillness as she knelt next to me. Her leg brushed against mine, the woodsy scent of her cloak whooshed over me, and the warmth of her hand soaked into my arm.

For a long moment, I couldn't breathe. She placed a fluttering hand upon my chest and then bent her ear near my mouth, clearly worried about my lack of breath. She drew close enough that her ear brushed my lips.

"I'm relieved to know you like me," I whispered, unable to contain my grin any longer.

She gasped and jumped back.

In an instant, my attacker was at her side, his knife unsheathed and pointed against my heart.

I ignored the man and stared up into Juliana's luscious brown eyes. "Hi there, sweetheart," I said with an expanding smile. "Aren't you a sight for sore eyes."

She scowled at me. "How long have you been awake?"

"It's nice to see you too."

"Did you see the entrance?" the peasant demanded, digging the tip of his knife so that it pierced my chest. I couldn't keep from flinching.

"Bulldog!" Juliana knocked the man's beefy hand away, sending the knife twirling to the hard-packed earth. "I told you not to hurt him."

"And I told you I'm not," the man yelled back. "If a couple punches and pricks hurts His Royal Highness, then he better crawl back to his mama's lap where he'll be safe."

I chuckled, the movement rattling my sore ribs. I nodded at Bulldog. I had a feeling I was going to like this feisty man, but I also knew that I would have to work hard to earn his trust.

The warmth of my blood seeped into my tunic, turning the fabric a brown-red and drawing Juliana's attention. "Now look what you did," she cried out, and pressed her fingers against my newest wound. "That was deeper than a prick."

Bulldog muttered under his breath, shook his head, and then stomped away.

Juliana ripped the edge of her tunic, and before I could stop her she'd edged my shirt up to the spot above my ribs where Bulldog's knife cut me. She pressed the piece of ragged linen against the slash.

I sucked in a sharp breath. I wasn't sure if it was from the pain or from the fact that I was lying before her with my bare chest exposed and her hand upon it.

"I'm sorry," she whispered, staunching the flow of my blood. "Bulldog isn't too happy you followed me here."

"I thought he looked overjoyed."

"He always has more bark than bite." Her gaze flitted to the hard contours of my chest, her eyes widening before flying quickly back to my wound.

As much as I liked having her aid, I knew I was putting her into a compromising situation by lying before her half naked. I pried the piece of rag from her fingers, sat up, and let my tunic fall back down. "Bulldog is right. It's just a nick. I'll be fine." I glanced at Bulldog, who was still watching my every movement, his knife ready to throw should I attempt anything.

Yes, I was surely going to like Bulldog. "He'll stop hating me once I show him the purse of gold and jewels."

"I don't want your wealth." She sat back and folded her arms. She'd been gone from the castle for less than twenty-four hours and already her face was streaked with mud and soot.

"I told you that they were yours, and I'm not going back on my word."

"I won't hold you to our deal. 'Tis my fault that I didn't finish my week—"

I yanked the purse out of the secret pocket of my damp cloak and tossed it toward Bulldog, who was squatting in front of the fire. "This is Juliana's. But she's turning her nose up at it."

Bulldog captured it with a swipe of his hand. He glowered at both of us, his dark brows furrowing together into a menacing line. Then he pried at the knot on the pouch. When he spilled the contents to the ground, the cavern turned silent.

I slid the diamond necklace from my pocket. "Here's one more thing for your collection." I tossed the jewel to Bulldog.

The man caught the sparkling necklace and then let it dangle from his hand above the pile of coins. When he finally looked at me, his brow had arched.

I nodded at him solemnly.

Bulldog nodded back.

And somehow I knew I'd gained the man's approval, albeit barely. If only I could tell Bulldog he had nothing to worry about, that I wanted to keep Juliana safe more than anything. If only I could convince them all that the safest course was for her to return to the castle with me.

I was planning to stay and complete my part of the bargain, whether Juliana wanted me to or not. In fact, maybe I wouldn't leave until she decided to come back with me.

# Chapter
## 12

*"You left without saying good-bye,"* Collin whispered near my ear, making my stomach quiver.

He was sitting against the dirt wall next to me, in front of the fire. Its blazing warmth had finally dried our clothing.

"I didn't think you'd care," I said softly, conscious that Bulldog hadn't stopped watching me, always scowling and ready to spring at Collin. The others had finally fallen asleep, as was our normal custom during the daylight hours—except for times I went on special "hunting" trips.

"Of course I care." Collin's fingers brushed against my hand at my side. I was helpless to resist when he slid his fingers into mine and laced our hands together.

Heat shimmied from my hand to my arm and then to my heart, making my pulse sputter faster. I was tempted to turn and look into his eyes, realizing how much I loved looking into the green that sparkled with endless mirth.

I hadn't expected him to trail me back to Wessex land. Surely he realized by now that my presence in his home had only been a hassle and would eventually bring both of us trouble.

"Besides," he said, "I promised you that I'd come visit your home for a week to learn more about what life is really like for the peasants."

I shrugged. At the time I'd made the bargain, his visit had seemed like a good plan. But Bulldog had made it clear that, trusted or not, Collin wasn't welcome. He'd demanded that the young nobleman be blindfolded at nightfall and taken far from our cave homes.

Part of me wanted to agree with Bulldog. My wise friend was only doing what he thought was best for all of us. But now, with Collin's fingers intertwined in mine, I wasn't sure I could let him go.

"Won't Lady Irene be worried about you," I asked, "and send out a search party?"

"I told her I was escorting you home, and that I would likely be gone a week."

I let my shoulders sink back against the chilly earth wall. Surely no one would suspect anything if he stayed. What harm could befall us?

"And why would I want to return home?" he whispered, humor edging his voice. "Not when I received such a friendly reception. I wouldn't want to miss my chance at having a few more ribs broken."

"Bulldog told me you didn't resist him or defend yourself."

"That's because, every once in a while, I like being beat up by angry peasants."

I smiled and nudged my shoulder playfully against his. "Are you ever serious?"

His fingers tightened against mine. In the darkness of the underground cave, the flickering flames of the fire cast a glow over his face and lit up his eyes. "I'm serious when I say I'd allow myself to be thrashed any day in order to see you."

Had he let Bulldog capture him and almost kill him, just so he could be with me? "You're crazy," I whispered.

"Not half as crazy as you," he whispered back. His arm pressed against mine, so that the hard length of his muscles rippled against me, reminding me of the smooth, defined contours of his chest I'd seen earlier when tending his wound.

I'd merely reacted to the sight of blood and hadn't stopped to think when I'd pulled up his tunic. I'd tended plenty of wounds for my friends in the past. But I'd never reacted to seeing their bare flesh the same way I had Collin's. He'd been noble to sense my discomfort and pull his garment back down.

The crackle of the fire filled the comfortable silence between us, along with the soft snores of my companions who were spread out on pallets around the fire.

Collin stifled a yawn.

"Why don't you sleep for a little while?" I suggested.

"If I close my eyes, I'm afraid Bulldog will slit my throat," he retorted dryly, glancing at the bulky frame of my protector.

Bulldog had finally closed his eyes, but I could tell from the uneven rise and fall of his chest he hadn't fallen asleep and likely wouldn't as long as Collin was there. "He's a good man. A second father to me."

"I think his son likes me even less." Collin glanced to where Thatch lay sprawled on his mat next to me, his eyelashes resting against his thin, freckled cheeks.

Thatch had scowled at Collin almost as fiercely as Bulldog had. The poor boy blamed Collin for the whipping Bulldog had given him when he'd returned home without me last week. I didn't begrudge the boy his anger.

"He'll forgive you once he gets to know you better," I said.

"He's besotted with you, that's clear enough," Collin said. "And I think he's jealous because you like me more than him."

"Thatch is only a boy."

"A boy on the cusp of manhood. A boy who's beginning to see you as the beautiful woman you are."

Was that true? Thatch's straw-colored hair poked out from his cap, which he wore even in sleep. He'd grown taller of late, so that his braies rose above his knees. And his toes poked through holes in the worn leather of boots devoid of laces that had long-past rotted away.

"I feel sorry for him," Collin said in a low voice. "You broke his heart when you fell in love with me."

My gaze swung to Collin as fast as the flap of a bat's wing. *Fell in love with him?*

I couldn't deny that I'd done nothing but think about him since the moment I'd slipped over the walls of his castle. After running for hours, I'd finally picked up the trail of one of our hunters and caught a ride back to camp with him. But through the dark hours of the night, images of Collin had haunted my every step.

Bulldog had greeted me with yells and snarls, but his shoulders had sagged with tangible relief and his eyes had brimmed with all the love he had for me. Yet even back in the security of his care, along with the glad embraces of my people, my heart had ached. I hadn't understood the longings, hadn't been able to make sense of the confusion stirring my discontent. Until now.

"So you have fallen in love with me," Collin teased. "At least you're not denying it."

"Of course I'm not in love with you," I whispered hotly, pulling my hand out of his grip. "I barely know you."

"You know me well enough." His voice dropped a notch.

"I know that you're terribly arrogant if you think I'd fall in love with someone like you."

He gave a soft chuckle that was altogether too self-confident.

"You're a nobleman," I hissed. "And I could never love a nobleman."

"That's too bad," he said lightly. "Because I'm pretty sure that I'm falling in love with you."

At his whispered confession, my breath caught in my throat. I couldn't move, couldn't think, couldn't formulate any kind of coherent response.

When his fingers found mine again and closed around my hand, my heart finally pounded forward again, but at double the speed. I didn't pull away. I didn't want to.

Strangely, I felt I was back where I needed to be. I let my fingers mingle with his and nestled my hand deep into his strong palm.

"You left this," he said, reaching for my other hand and sliding a thick ring onto my thumb. The polished silver contained the warmth of the finger where he'd worn it.

"It's yours," I said, but I didn't make an effort to remove it.

"I gave it to you. And I want you to have it." There was a possessiveness in his voice that settled deep into my soul. And when he wrapped his strong fingers around my hand, holding it with the other, I didn't resist. In fact, I let my body slump against him, suddenly tired but happier than I could remember being in a long time.

I didn't want to think about anything too deeply. I just wanted to savor the moment of being with him again. With a soft sigh, I rested my head against his shoulder. And when he pressed a gentle kiss against my cap, it felt as if it were the most natural action in the world.

I didn't know what was happening to me. All I knew was that I couldn't send him away as Bulldog wanted. Not that night.

Maybe not ever.

I DIDN'T HAVE THE HEART TO TELL JULIANA THAT HER blindfold wouldn't stop me from retracing my steps and finding the secret passageway if I wanted.

"Are we there yet?" I asked.

She gave me a playful push. "You're worse than a child. You've asked me that a hundred times already."

"And that's why you love me," I teased back.

She didn't say anything.

I grinned and drew hope from her silence. At least she hadn't denied me again. And she hadn't given me back my ring. She was still wearing it on the thumb where I'd lodged it, even though Bulldog had raised his brow at the sight of it there.

We'd dozed and talked all afternoon and evening, sitting against the dirt wall holding hands. Then, after night had fallen, Juliana had blindfolded me and we'd slipped quietly out of the underground hovel. Apparently, sometime during the day Bulldog changed his mind about allowing me to stay. For how long, I didn't know. I didn't care. I'd take all the time with Juliana I could get.

"It's my turn to show you what a real party is like," she said from behind me, her hand upon my back and guiding me through the thick brush.

When we reached a small clearing, she untied my blindfold, revealing a bonfire and a gathering of at least fifty women and children. Some of the women were busy cooking over large pots, others were kneeling at a nearby stream scrubbing and laundering their pitiful rags of clothing by the low light of the fire. The children were running around, many of them barefooted in the cold temperature of the autumn night.

Over the open firepit, several men were in the process of roasting a boar, turning the spit and laughing together. The dripping juices and wafting scent indicated the meal was almost ready.

I blinked back my astonishment at the number of assembled peasants as Juliana stepped next to me, taking in the gathering with a smile.

"How many live here?" I asked, my gaze alighting upon a young boy with a missing leg limping on a crude crutch.

"We're up to about eighty." Her smile disappeared as she surveyed the gathering with more seriousness. "Every week, we grow. And it becomes more difficult to feed and clothe everyone."

A posse of men led by Bulldog came into the clearing from another direction. They were armed and carried several crates between them.

"I imagine it's getting more difficult to stay hidden from your uncle too."

She nodded. "That's why we only come out after dark. We make sure everyone is back in the caves before dawn breaks."

She didn't have the chance to say more. The children had spotted her and scampered over. At first they cowered away from me, clutching Juliana and receiving her kind words and tender embraces.

"I'll let you do the honor," she said, tossing me her sack. "Since you're the one providing for my friends tonight."

I pried open the drawstring to reveal figs, apples, a dozen hard rolls, and a large wedge of cheese. "I see you took a detour to the kitchen on the way out of my castle."

"You must thank Lord Collin for his generosity," she told the children, all the while grinning at me.

I smiled in return, but as I began to hand out the food items to the children, an ache formed in the pit of my stomach. Their faces were too thin, their fingers too eager as they clasped their treasures. And as they devoured their meager gifts, their wide eyes filled with fear of me, almost as if they were afraid I'd snatch back the food before they could finish.

The sick gnawing inside me only grew throughout the feast that ensued. I wanted to refuse the slab of greasy pork that someone passed to me and tell them to divide my portion among the children. But Juliana's headshake warned me against it. They were tolerating me because of her, even though their wary glances told me they'd much rather that I leave. Refusing their generosity would be like a slap in the face.

I only wished I'd thought to grab a couple of sacks of food on my way out of the castle as well. I could have brought some of the bundles of provisions that Juliana and I had put together for the poor tenants on my land. It clearly wouldn't have been enough. But it would have been more than they had now.

When I noticed that Juliana had given away her portions, I pushed my half-eaten pork into her hands. "Eat mine," I insisted.

She glanced at the tender pink meat and nibbled her bottom lip. I didn't care if I offended anyone by giving away my meal. I couldn't bear to think that she'd go hungry.

"I ate enough at the dance to fill my belly for a week," I joked, even as my stomach gurgled with the pangs of hunger.

"You're sure?" she asked, peering up at me with round, trusting eyes.

I'd already taken a couple of bites and wanted to ravage it the way the other men were eating theirs. But I pushed the pork toward her, forcing her to keep it. "I'm absolutely sure. Now eat it."

Without another moment of hesitation, she tore into the meat.

Over her bent head, my gaze connected with Bulldog's. The man was gnawing a bone clean, but paused and nodded his approval at the sacrifice I'd made.

My chest swelled with strange satisfaction. I'd never had to make sacrifices before. Sure, I was finally giving something to my poor tenants and had instructed William to carry forth the delivery plans without me. But I hadn't suffered as a result. The giving hadn't really been much of a sacrifice due to my immense wealth.

However, tonight, I'd given something that, simple as it was, had cost me. I'd go hungry as a result. For a reason I couldn't explain, I was more fulfilled than if I'd given away another diamond necklace.

After eating every morsel of the boar, one peasant man who'd had his eyes gouged out by Lord Wessex started a lively tune on his battered fiddle. Even though he couldn't see, a gaping grin split his leathery face as he stared blankly at the men and women who were stomping and laughing and twirling.

Juliana pushed me into the mix, and soon I found myself laughing along with her as I stumbled to learn dances that were much livelier than anything I'd ever danced.

Breathless and laughing, I finally pulled Juliana to the fringe of the circle.

"Are we wearing you out, my lord?" she asked with a smile that was as wide and beautiful as the cloudless sky overhead.

"You could never wear me out." I meant my words to be light and playful, but they came out filled with more longing than I intended.

Strands of her hair had come loose, and I wished I had the freedom to take her cap, toss it into the blazing fire, and burn it for good. I longed to see her curls spill over her shoulders and twirl as she danced. In fact, I wanted to pull her into my arms, bury my fingers in her hair, and let them get tangled there.

As if sensing the direction of my thoughts, her smile faded and her pupils widened. Her lips parted just slightly, and I could hear her intake of breath, almost as if she were waiting for me to draw her near.

Did I dare?

I started to reach for her, but a sudden flare from a burning arrow came from the distant forest and landed in the midst of the dancers.

Juliana's body tensed.

"What is it?" I asked.

"Our perimeter guard has spotted someone," she said tersely.

The dancers stopped. The music screeched to a halt. And the children ceased their giggling and games. A terrible silence fell over the clearing, and all eyes fixed upon the burning arrow.

Then, before anyone could speak or react, Juliana strode toward the center of the circle. "This is the sign that it is time to end our feasting," she said evenly and quietly to the group. "Remember, you must not leave a trace of evidence that we've been here, and you must stay on the deer paths as you return to safety."

With her calm words of instruction, the peasants followed her lead in gathering their supplies, putting out the fire, burying the ashes, and covering the pit with windfall. Although an urgency filled their whispers, Juliana managed to keep everyone from panicking.

"You need to blindfold His Royal Highness," Bulldog ordered Juliana as we raced along an invisible deer path.

I stopped to pick up the crippled boy with a crutch at the same time that Juliana hefted a lagging child to her hip.

"A blindfold won't stop me from finding your secret passageway," I admitted, sliding the lame boy to my back and slinging another small child across my shoulders.

Bulldog muttered under his breath, but stooped to assist an urchin in our race back to the caverns. Juliana sprinted ahead of us, disappearing into the darkness of the night.

"I hope you know," I spoke over my shoulder to Bulldog, "I only want to keep Juliana safe."

"Then leave. Now."

"I want her to come with me."

Bulldog growled. "She's not going anywhere."

I stumbled over a twig and strained to right myself. The two children clung to my cloak and the wool pulled against my throat, nearly choking me. But I jogged forward anyway, attempting to distinguish the path by the faint light of the moon.

"Do you want her running like this forever?" I managed. "This is no way to live. She'll be better off and safer with me, and you know it." A low twig whipped my face, stinging my skin, but I plunged forward anyway.

For several long seconds, Bulldog didn't say anything. The crunch of our boots and our labored breathing were the only sounds that surrounded us.

When Bulldog finally spoke, his voice was harsh. "What are your intentions toward her?"

My intentions? I almost tripped. What would I do with Juliana if I took her back to my home? "I love her," I stated simply. And it was the truth.

"If you want her," Bulldog said, "then you'll make her your wife first."

*Wife?* I liked the sound of that. True, maybe she wasn't the kind of woman I'd imagined I'd have by my side for the rest of my life. I supposed I'd always pictured myself with some-one more like Lady Rosemarie—the fair-haired, beautiful lady whose heart I'd tried to win the past summer.

But perhaps Juliana was more suited toward me. She was bolder, braver, and clever enough to withstand my humor and playfulness. In fact, she had no trouble putting me in my place. I loved her quick wit and strength.

Yes, Juliana was the woman for me.

"I'll marry her," I said over my shoulder. "As my wife, she'll never have to fear Lord Wessex again."

"You'll keep her safe, or I'll come kill you myself."

I chuckled. "You won't need to worry about that. She'll never want for anything ever again."

Bulldog grunted. And I knew the matter was settled. My pulse thrummed with new excitement.

I was going to marry Juliana Wessex.

# Chapter
# 13

*I pulled the hemp cord of my bow taut. The sleek* arrow with its feathered end fit between my fingers before I released the shaft into the blackness of the forest. Within seconds, the swift twang indicated I'd hit the mark.

"Dead center," called one of the men who stood near the target.

I smiled triumphantly and turned to face Collin.

By the light of torches, he was a bronzed and rugged. His blond hair swirled over his forehead above his gleaming green eyes, and his lips curved to form a breathtaking grin.

"Let's see if you can do better than that, my lord," I said, standing back and waving at the spot I'd vacated.

"I don't really think this is fair." He peered through the darkness of the night.

"He's scared," Thatch said hotly. "His Royal Highness is scared."

Collin bowed with the mock regality of a king, having endured the nickname with his usual grace and wit. Even though Collin had proven himself over the past week of living among us, Thatch still treated Collin like the enemy.

I'd been more than a little surprised when Collin joined in every activity as if he were one of us. He'd hunted, hauled water from the creek, and chopped wood without complaint. The children had quickly lost their fear of him and flocked to him for his teasing and grins and playfulness. Even Bulldog had stopped glaring at him.

Collin reached over and tousled Thatch's already bristly hair. "I *am* scared. You have archery contests in the dark all the time. You're used to this. But I on the other hand . . ."

Thatch batted Collin's arm away and stepped back with a scowl. "You couldn't hit the side of a deer even if it ran in front of you and asked you to shoot it."

Collin laughed.

I narrowed my eyes upon Thatch. I hoped my young friend would read the message, that he needed to stop being so spiteful. But Thatch only shifted his face away from me, his sullenness even more pronounced than yesterday. Perhaps Collin had been correct in his assessment that Thatch was jealous.

We'd been like brother and sister for many years, even before my father had been killed and we'd had to flee to the forest. Thatch had always been my ready accomplice. He trailed me everywhere. He'd always told me he'd protect me.

And now Collin was stepping in and taking my attention.

"Maybe I need a few lessons," Collin said, winking at me. "And since Juliana is obviously the best one here, I elect her to show me how it's done."

"The only lessons you need are ones in humility," I replied, thinking back to the archery contest Collin had held and how he'd pretended to give me lessons. The idea of doing the same to him sent a shiver of pleasure through me.

"Since I'm such a terrible archer," Collin said with sparkling eyes, "why don't you blindfold me. If I am to lose, I might as well lose big."

The other men guffawed. One produced a strip of cloth and tied it over Collin's eyes.

Although Collin seemed to be enjoying himself now, he'd been reluctant to allow anyone to leave the underground cavern earlier that night, wanting us to stay inside while he investigated the region for signs he'd spotted of another intruder. I'd informed him that Uncle always had his soldiers out looking for us. We were accustomed to having to return to hiding at night when a soldier was spotted. Even with our assurances, Collin had taken time to scour the perimeter of our forest home before joining us for the archery contest.

I had no doubt Collin was more skilled than he was letting on. I'd witnessed his accuracy before. But in the forest, in the dark? Blindfolded?

He took his position, faced the target, and after standing for several long moments, he pulled the string swiftly and released his arrow. When Jack, the peasant man at the target, called out that Collin's arrow hit dead center, I was as speechless as the other men.

Collin only laughed and challenged me again.

"I must see for myself," I called, striding to the hidden target. "Perhaps you've paid our judge a purse of gold to rule in your favor."

Collin started after me. "Maybe it was beginner's luck."

I trotted through the maze of trees and brush, dodging twigs and jumping over fallen branches until I reached the rings we'd painted on a bag stuffed with straw.

"Hit it fair and square," Jack said, his gap-toothed grin radiating admiration toward Collin. "Right same spot too."

In the darkness, I slid my fingers along the target until I found Collin's arrow hole. It was slightly more on center than mine.

Collin's breathing came over my shoulder and his arm brushed past mine. His fingers groped for the indentation on the target as well. "See, I told you I didn't cheat," his voice rumbled near my ear.

"Then I guess you do have beginner's luck." At his nearness, my breath came out choppy.

Collin cocked his head at Jack, who remained near the target. "Go back and tell the others that we tied. Juliana and I shall move the target back a dozen more feet and have a rematch. This time we'll straddle the high branch of the oak."

Jack gave a cheer and then raced off.

But Collin didn't move. He remained where he was behind me, boxing me in with his arms. His mouth brushed my ear. "All week, I've been dying to find a way to be alone with you."

I shivered with pleasure. "We shouldn't be alone."

"Just for a minute," he whispered. Then he pressed his lips to my cheek. The warmth and softness of his kiss melted me, and I leaned backward into him. All traces of protest vanished.

"Remember when I told you I was falling in love with you?" he asked.

How could I forget? I hadn't been able to think of much else.

"Well, I thought more about it." He slipped his arms around my waist and drew me against him so that I rested in his arms, my back pressed firmly against his chest. "And I'm not falling in love with you."

"You're not?" I twisted my head so that I could see the outline of his face.

"No, I'm not *falling* in love. I'm *already* in love."

"Oh." The whispered word contained an embarrassing amount of relief.

In the faint moonlight, his smile had the power to render me speechless. "I love you, Juliana."

The words drifted into me, warm and sweet, like the gentlest summer breeze, caressing my heart and whispering into my blood.

He searched my face. Was he looking for my response there?

I'd never met anyone like Collin, never experienced the depth of emotions I was having with him. After being with him all week here in the forest, I certainly couldn't deny my attraction to him. But was this love?

He leaned in and his breath bathed my cheek.

I tilted my head back. If he wanted to kiss me again, I wouldn't stop him.

His breath lingered above my lips for several long, sweet moments, and then he captured my mouth with his. His soft fullness moved against mine setting fireflies to flight in my stomach.

He broke away all too quickly, leaving me trembling and wishing for more.

I knew I should twist my face away, shouldn't give him the chance to kiss me again, but I couldn't move. And when he lifted a hand and smoothed his fingers over my cheek, I closed my eyes and basked in his love.

"Marry me." His whisper was followed by a kiss to my forehead.

His words were so soft that at first I wasn't sure if I'd heard him correctly.

"I want to marry you, Juliana," he said louder, pulling back just slightly.

At his declaration, my eyes flew open, and I stiffened.

"I talked with Bulldog," he rushed, his words urgent. "And he's given me permission to ask for your hand in marriage."

I started to shake my head, but the earnestness in his expression stopped me.

"Please, Juliana. Let me make you my wife and take you away from here."

Tomorrow would be the end of his weeklong agreement. Although he hadn't made any mention of leaving and I hadn't wanted to bring it up, it was inevitable that he'd have to depart sometime. "Collin—" I started.

He pressed a finger to my lips to stop my protest. "You don't belong here. You belong with me, where you'll be safe and where I can take care of you the way you deserve."

The snap of a nearby twig broke through my conscience. I jerked out of Collin's arms.

There, only feet away, stood Thatch. He glared at us, his gaze bouncing back and forth between Collin and me. Hurt mingled with the stiff anger that twisted his boney features.

"Oh, I see how it is," Thatch said, his voice tight. "You meet *him*, and now we're not good enough for you anymore."

"That's not true," I said, reaching for my friend.

But Thatch took a step away, his eyes shooting sharp arrows at my heart. "That's fine. You just go on and marry him. I don't care."

"Thatch," I admonished.

But he'd moved several more paces away from me. "Go on. Get out of here." The boy's voice cracked with his emotion. Through the moonlight, I glimpsed the tears streaking his cheeks. "Just leave with your fancy nobleman. And good riddance."

Before I could stop him or say anything more, he crashed into the brush and ran away.

I chased after him, calling him to stop, but he plunged farther into the thick brush. Finally, I stopped, my shoulders slumping as discouragement settled over me.

"He'll come around eventually." Collin had followed after me and stared at the spot in the dark woodland where Thatch had disappeared. "If he loves you, then he'll realize, like Bulldog, that you'll have a better life with me."

"I can't leave them." The words fell from my lips before I could think. But once they were out, the painful truth hit me in the chest.

"They understand that this is no place for you." Collin waved his hands at the dark forest and the lurking shadows. "I'm taking you home with me."

"This is my home," I stated. "And these peasants are my family now."

"I know you've grown attached to them over the years. But you don't belong here."

"Where do I belong, Collin?" My voice contained all the frustration that had built during the past couple of weeks of experiencing both worlds, and of realizing that Collin had shattered my carefully crafted stereotype of all noblemen. He'd indeed won our bargain. "I don't fit in with the nobility anymore. When I was staying with you, everyone knew I was different, that I wasn't comfortable there."

"You'll adjust. It's just been a while."

I shook my head. "I don't want to adjust. After living this way and seeing the suffering of my friends, how could I ever return to living in comfort and wealth?"

"But that's what you were born to. It's your birthright. Nobility is in your blood."

"I couldn't live with a full stomach knowing my friends are starving. I couldn't live in warmth knowing they're freezing. And I couldn't dress up in fancy gowns when I know they're dressed in mere rags."

He didn't answer me except to wrench off his cap and stick his fingers in his hair. The battle raging across his features tore at me.

"I have to stay and help them."

"We can find another way to ease their suffering." His voice was laced with desperation.

"I won't abandon them. They rely upon me."

"They'll get along without you. They have Bulldog."

"I can't let them—let him—face my uncle alone." I bowed my head. "Not when it's my fault and the fault of my father that they have to live as outcasts in the forest."

He reached for my hands. "It's not your fault, Juliana." I relished the strength of his fingers upon mine. But it only made my heart ache all the more. "If my father hadn't started the peasant uprising, they wouldn't have joined him and become outlaws. If only my father had just been content to live in peace, they'd all still be safe in their homes instead of living in the forest in caves."

Collin shook his head. "You can't blame your father or yourself. Your uncle is a cruel man, and he would have treated them poorly regardless of the uprising. You yourself have spoken of his continued greed and unfair tax laws."

"But many of the laws are a result of my father's actions. My uncle is punishing the people because of his rebellion."

"Your uncle is punishing the people because he's a beast—"

I pulled out of his grip. "I have to stay and help right the wrongs."

"And stealing a few petty jewels from helpless noblemen and women is the answer?" His expression had darkened with frustration.

"At least it fills the bellies of my friends."

"And for how long? How long do you expect that you can go on like this, hiding in the woods and dressing as the Cloaked Bandit?"

"As long as God allows it," I retorted, although deep inside I wasn't so sure God approved of what I was doing in the first place.

"Bulldog knows as well as I do that it's only a matter of time before Lord Wessex catches you. And when he discovers you're a woman *and* his long-lost niece, he'll flay you alive."

Our voices had risen with the emotion of the argument. I knew the others would hear us and soon be upon us to discover what was wrong.

"I can't marry you, Collin."

"And I can't let you stay here and put your life at risk."

"It's my choice."

He narrowed his eyes. "I'll sling you over my shoulder and carry you away from here if I have to."

"I'll just run away again." I glared at him.

He glared back.

Bulldog burst through the shrubs and nearly barreled into us. He held a hunting knife in both hands and his face was scrunched into a fierce scowl.

"What's going on?" he demanded, glancing around.

I couldn't answer him. And Collin's jaw flexed with his silence.

The others broke through the woodland, their weapons drawn, their faces creased with worry.

"Is he hurting you?" Bulldog jumped at Collin, grabbed him by the neck, and angled his knife against the bulging vein there.

"No!" I cried out.

But Bulldog didn't budge. His heavy breathing testified to his haste in coming to my rescue.

Even though Bulldog was tough and mean, he loved me. I couldn't leave him. Not after all he'd done for me over the years.

"I was proposing to Juliana," Collin offered. "But apparently she's determined to stay here."

Bulldog's hand fell away. His small, round eyes bored into me and seemed to ask if I was certain.

I nodded. "This is my life now. I don't belong in that world anymore."

Bulldog glanced between me and Collin, studying both of us. Then finally, he shrugged. "I won't force you to go."

There was something in his tone that told me he thought I'd be safer with Collin. But I knew he spoke truly—he wouldn't make me do something I didn't want to do.

Collin stared at me. But I refused to meet his gaze. I was too afraid that if I looked into his eyes again and saw his love and longing, I wouldn't be able to resist him.

Silence stretched among our group. A cold breeze rustled through the branches, and it seeped through the layers of my cloak and sent chills up my arms. I ignored the ache in my chest and pushed away all thoughts of being with Collin. He lived the kind of opulent life I was fighting against. And even though I'd noticed he was growing in compassion for the poor and would perhaps even become a benevolent ruler of his lands, I could never be with him. We were worlds apart. And as far as I could see, those worlds couldn't be bridged.

I took a deep breath and forced myself to think rationally, as I always had. I steeled my chin and shoulders. Then I slipped his ring from my thumb, approached him, and thrust it into his hand. "I don't love you, Collin, and I never will."

Collin's back slumped and the air swooshed from his lungs, almost as if someone had pummeled a fist into his stomach.

Even if I didn't love him, I did care about him. Deeply. Perhaps even deeper than I wanted to admit to myself. But by saying the hurtful words, I would drive him away. And his leaving would be for the best. I couldn't drag him into my battles. This was no way of life for anyone. If I must live it, I would do it without bringing harm to him.

It would be best for both of us if he went away and we pretended we'd never met.

Sadness creased the corners of his eyes as his fingers closed around the ring.

I stepped back, not quite sure why it hurt so much to release the ring into his hold.

"I guess I should say my good-byes," he said hoarsely.

"Yes, I guess you should."

"Then good-bye, Juliana."

"Good-bye, my lord."

When he turned to walk away, I was unprepared for the sudden ripping in my chest. With every step he took, I realized he carried my heart with him, leaving a painful gaping emptiness in its place.

# Chapter 14

I SAT WITH MY HEAD DOWN ON THE DESK. THE WIND howled through the cracks in the shutters barring the windows. Errant drips of rain came in through the chimney and sizzled against the low fire.

I didn't care that the solar had grown steadily colder over the night and into the creeping light of a new day. I didn't care that my stomach ached with hunger pangs. I didn't care that I'd been sitting in the same spot since I'd arrived home nearly twenty-four hours ago.

I couldn't make myself care about anything.

All I could think about was that I'd lost Juliana. That she hadn't loved me. That she hadn't wanted to be with me.

I groaned and stared again at the ring she'd given back.

At first, anger had driven me. I'd stomped my way out of Wessex forest fuming and muttering, aghast that she'd had the pluck to turn down my proposal and send me away. I'd told myself it was for the best, that if she was so determined to scrounge around like a wild beast, I'd let her.

But the farther away from her I'd run, the more my anger dissipated. Until finally, when I'd reached the castle gatehouse, every trace of fury had blown away only to be replaced with a throbbing pain.

And now . . . that dull ache festered in my heart.

"Juliana," I whispered, my throat dry. I'd made myself nearly sick every time I thought of her sitting up in a tree, ready to jump behind another nobleman and rob him of a few jewels. Her stunt had been fine—even humorous—when I'd been the nobleman getting robbed. But I grew ill at the image of her attempting the dangerous feat on anyone else. With a frustrated shout, I jumped to my feet and let my chair clatter to the floor behind me. I drew in a breath, released it . . . then threw my ring with all my might. It flew across the room, pinged against the door, and skittered back across the floor, rolling to a stop in the middle of the room.

I'd rather die than let any harm befall her. I couldn't—wouldn't—stay in my castle while she put her life in danger at every turn. What other choice did I have but to go back and drag her away from the forest? I'd haul her into one of the towers and lock her there until she promised not to run away.

With stiff limbs, I started toward the door. But when I reached it, instead of pulling it open I stopped and rested my forehead against the carved paneling. How could I force her to live here? She'd only grow to hate me. And how could I bear that?

I spun and glanced around the room, my heart racing with a need to do something, anything. I couldn't sit at my counting table, locked away in my solar—not while she was out facing only God knew what trouble. If I stayed any longer, I'd go crazy.

My gaze landed upon the open ledger, the quill pen lying discarded next to an open ink pot. I narrowed my eyes upon the black blotch at the bottom of the page where William had carelessly left the pen.

The figures told of wealth, of a fortune vaster than any other in this area. Surely I could use some of my riches to provide for Juliana and the peasants displaced by Lord Wessex. Perhaps even move the peasants to Goodrich land, build them homes, and provide them with food and clothing. And if I brought them to my land, I could keep them safe from Lord Wessex. I could watch over Juliana and make sure Wessex never threatened her again.

My pulse slowed to a rational speed, and I took a gulp of air to calm my breathing. Bringing Juliana and her people onto Goodrich land was the perfect solution. I'd be able to give them all the food and provisions that they needed, especially with winter coming soon.

I opened the door, my blood pumping harder, my mind growing clearer. "William! Come at once!" My trusted steward would know what to do.

I started back toward my desk, my steps surer, the panic in my gut loosening. For several minutes, I studied the figures on the pages of the ledger, attempting to make sense of them. When the door squeaked open farther, I exhaled my relief. "William, I need your help."

"William isn't here." At my sister's quiet statement, I glanced up. She stood in the doorway, her hands clasped tightly in front of her, her thin face drawn. Her gown was wrinkled and her usual neat plait was unkempt and fuzzy, as though she'd slept fully clothed and had yet to groom herself for the day.

"Send for him. I need him right away." I pushed aside the discarded pen and frowned at the inky mess William had left on the ledger. The man was clumsy, but when it came to the books, he was usually meticulous.

Irene didn't move from the doorway. "William is gone."

At the unnatural tone of her voice, my gaze snapped up. "You mean he's dead?"

She lowered her head and stared at the slipper poking from beneath the hem of her skirt. "I don't know."

A shiver of trepidation crept up my spine, but I straightened my shoulders and braced myself for a fight. "Stop speaking in ambiguities and explain yourself."

She visibly swallowed. "Lord Wessex's sheriff has taken William away for questioning."

For a moment I almost didn't believe I'd heard Irene correctly. But at the slump of her shoulders, another shiver lifted the hairs at the back of my neck. "Lord Wessex's sheriff has taken my most trusted servant? For questioning?"

Irene nodded.

"And why is he questioning William?" But even as I asked the question, a knot of dread twisted in my stomach.

"He was curious about Lady Eleanora Delacroix."

My heartbeat slammed into my ribs. "And just what did Lord Wessex want to know?"

"She seemed familiar to him."

"And . . ."

"And after much prying, he discovered that there is no one named Lady Eleanora Delacroix visiting these lands."

My fingers tightened into a fist. "Then he's badly mistaken."

"It wasn't hard to figure out, Collin."

"You told him?" I clenched my jaw together to keep from yelling.

Irene lifted her chin. "I didn't tell him anything that he wouldn't have figured out on his own, with time." Her eyes flashed with a defiance that made my heart sink. I knew she'd been angry with me because I'd denied her request to speak with Lord Wessex about a union with Edgar. But surely she hadn't betrayed me while I was gone. With slow, even steps, I crossed the room until I towered above her. "And what did you tell Lord Wessex?" My voice was low in an attempt to contain my anger.

Her gaze wavered. "Just my suspicions. That's all."

"And what exactly are your suspicions?"

"You dragged her here in the middle of the night. She was disguised as a peasant in men's clothing. You had several servants remake Mother's garments for her because she came with nothing of her own. And then you offered her a pouch of gold to stay for the week. But in interacting with her, it was clear that she's not a peasant but rather a fine lady and a very fine archer."

"What else did you tell Lord Wessex?" I demanded.

"He wanted to know which of the servants would be able to answer his further questions about your guest. So I told him Mistress Higgins and William were the only servants you'd allowed to have contact with the woman."

"That scoundrel had his sheriff take Mistress Higgins too?" My muscles tightened. "You do know he'll torture them both mercilessly to get the information he wants."

A flicker of remorse fell across Irene's features, and she lowered her head. "I didn't think he'd take them with him." Her voice deflated. "I only thought he would question them here before he left."

"That's right. You didn't think. You reacted in childish anger toward me and thought to hurt me by tainting Lady Eleanora's reputation. And now you have brought harm upon two of our most loyal and trusted servants instead."

Her head dipped lower. "You wouldn't let me have Edgar. I only wanted to expose her for a fraud and show you how it felt to be denied what you want. I didn't think I'd bring danger to our servants."

And she'd brought untold danger to Juliana as well. Surely after extracting fragments of information from both Mistress Higgins and William, Wessex would discover that his niece was still alive. After all, William had been on the tower when Juliana had shared the details of her past. Even if he hadn't heard our entire conversation, certainly parts of it had reached his ears.

No matter how loyal William was, there were torture methods that could make even the staunchest man talk.

"I shall have to go to Wessex now and retrieve them." I retraced my steps to the desk, my body tensing in readiness for the task before me. "And hopefully I'll arrive before his torturing kills them."

Along the way, I'd have to warn Juliana that Wessex had likely discovered who she was. I'd take the blame squarely upon myself. And if she hadn't loved me before, she would surely hate me now.

At least I could take comfort in the fact that Juliana was well hidden, that the caves were impossible to find. Even if William told everything, Lord Wessex would never be able to track her down.

I poked the embers of the fire with a stick, sending a shower of sparks into the air of the dank hovel. The rain had fallen endlessly through the night and into the morning. And now rivulets of cold water trickled down the walls, dampening the ground and making our home slick, cold, and unbearably muddy.

I knew I should try to get some sleep alongside the others who were sprawled out on the wet hay and damp pallets around the fire. But I hadn't been able to do much of anything since Collin had left more than a day ago.

Had I been foolish to send him away? The question clamored like a gong, growing louder with each hour.

Every part of my body ached with a strange longing for Collin. All yesterday and all last night, I'd watched for him, expected him to reappear. I kept glancing at the secret tunnel, hoping I'd see his blond head pop through the opening and his disarming grin flash at me.

His affirmation of love and his last tender kiss pulsed in my blood and pumped through every corner of my body, claiming me and stirring a desire for him. The need grew so strong at times that my chest hurt.

I couldn't deny that I cared about him, though not enough to leave behind all of the people who depended upon me. Even if I didn't have that responsibility, I still wouldn't be able to go with him. I despised the nobility, didn't I? And I wanted nothing to do with them. I'd cut myself off from that lifestyle forever, hadn't I? And I certainly didn't miss all of the comforts, the soft warm bed, the security of a dry room, and a steady supply of hot, filling food.

I glanced around the cave, the roots in the low ceiling hanging down and beginning to drip rainwater and squelched unfamiliar discontentment. My gaze slowed on Thatch's empty spot. He still hadn't returned after running away the night he'd caught me in Collin's arms, at the moment Collin had asked me to marry him.

I'd already discussed the situation with Bulldog, and we'd agreed if Thatch didn't return by noon, we would have to go outside the caves and track him down. Like Bulldog, I was praying he hadn't tried any robbery stunts or hunting on his own. It was one thing for me to occasionally poach or steal from an unsuspecting nobleman. But I certainly didn't want Thatch attempting it.

My attention shifted to Bulldog. He was lying on his pallet, eyes wide open, staring into the fire. His thick brows had formed into their usual thunderous position above his black eyes.

An uncomfortable niggling of guilt wormed its way through me. I had no doubt Bulldog reacted the same way whenever I went off on one of my reckless missions or hunting escapades. I worried him as much as Thatch worried me now.

"You should have gone with Lord Collin." Bulldog's gravelly whisper knocked into me, and for a moment, I was speechless at his gruff admission.

I shook my head. "I didn't want to."

"He'll be able to keep you safer and happier than I ever could."

"I don't care."

"He loves you."

"Well, I don't love him."

"Yes, you do," Bulldog whispered fiercely. "You're just too stubborn to admit it." He propped himself up on his elbows so that I had no choice but to look at the stubs of his missing thumbs. "Stop acting like a child, Juliana."

"I'm not."

He growled. "In case you haven't noticed, you're a full-grown woman now. And you can't live down here with a bunch of men forever."

My gaze touched on the dirty, bearded faces of the men who'd become my friends over the past couple of years. None of them had ever paid any attention to the fact that I was a girl. Why would they start now that I was getting older?

"If it worries you, then I'll start sleeping with the women and children."

"You have to get married eventually."

"Says who?"

"I do!" His voice thundered through the cavern. Several of the men stirred. Bulldog waited a few seconds, then continued in a lower voice. "Lord Collin is the kind of man your father would have picked for you if he was still alive."

"Collin's father offered a union when we were but children, and my father refused."

"That's because Lord Goodrich was a self-serving dog."

I shrugged.

"Collin Goodrich is not his father."

"I thought you said the only good nobleman was a dead one."

"Well, this one is good for something." Bulldog lowered his voice back to a rasp. "For taking you away from this pit."

My mind tumbled back over all the experiences I'd had with Collin: the constant kindness he'd shown to me, the generosity, the tenderness. He'd even humbled himself enough to live with me in the caverns. He hadn't required special treatment and had, in fact, attempted to learn as much as he could about our way of life, as well as adapt to mine.

Collin Goodrich was a decent, God-fearing man. Any woman would be blessed to have him as a husband.

A place deep inside me ached to be that woman.

Was Bulldog right? Did I love Collin?

Or was I merely growing more convicted of the wrongness of my stealing? I'd always felt justified. But what if God was displeased with my methods? Was He calling me to do something different? Something that wouldn't lower me to the same level as my uncle? Because that's what I'd done, hadn't I? I'd resorted to the same ugly tactics Uncle used.

A sudden noise in the hidden passageway brought Bulldog to his knees. He unsheathed his knife and had it ready to throw before my fingers even connected with mine. My heart lurched with sudden keen longing. I suddenly desperately prayed the noise was Collin, that he'd come back, that he would admit he couldn't leave my side.

Maybe he'd decided to stay with me in the forest.

I released a disappointed breath when the head that poked into the cavern belonged to one of the guards posted on duty above ground. "Thatch's come back," he whispered to Bulldog. "But he's hurt somethin' awful."

Bulldog re-sheathed his knife and scrambled on hands and knees through the winding maze of tunnels faster than I could keep up. When we finally reached the base of the large hollowed-out oak that hid the opening of our caves, I was breathing hard and my pulse hammered with worry.

I crawled through the splintered bark of the tree and ducked out into the thick woodland that shrouded the entrance to our homes. The steady patter of rain greeted me, along with the sight of Thatch propped against a nearby trunk.

He leaned his head back, giving a clear view of his battered face. His straw-like hair was plastered to his forehead above bruised eyes and cheeks. Blood dripped from his nose and ran with the rain onto his swollen and cracked lips.

Bulldog rushed forward and fell to his knees in front of his son. "What happened to you, boy?"

Thatch shook his head and glanced wildly behind him. He tried to turn, but instead cradled his arms to his chest.

When Bulldog pried one of his son's hands forward, Thatch cried out in pain. "Did you break your arm?" Bulldog asked.

I kneeled next to him. A glance at his hands told me he'd experienced much more than a broken arm. His fingers were bloodied, the tips punctured, his fingernails torn from the flesh.

The skin on my back prickled. My fingers closed around my knife, then went to the bare spot on my shoulder where my bow would have been had I not rushed out of the cave without it.

"He's been tortured," I whispered. But even as I spoke the words, Bulldog slipped out his dagger.

I'd seen enough torture and mistreatment over the years that the blood and gore didn't rile my stomach. It only fueled my anger. "Who would do such a thing? And why?"

The soft whinny of a horse came from behind me. "I did it."

I stiffened and tightened my grip around the knife.

"Drop your weapons or I'll kill the boy," came the low voice.

Bulldog's forehead furrowed into deep crevices and his eyes narrowed. Slowly, he lowered his dagger as he spun to face the intruder.

I followed his example, unwilling to put Thatch in any further danger.

At the sight that met me, my blood turned as cold as the rain that was pelting my head.

There, on a pure white steed and wearing a white cloak, sat Lord Wessex. Another horse stepped out of the shadows, carrying Edgar. He gave a pointed glance around the woods at the wide circle of soldiers surrounding us, their bows stretched with arrows notched. All of them pointed at me. "We offer you our sincerest greetings," Edgar said.

"And my deepest thanks to your boy for so kindly leading the way here," Uncle said to Bulldog. "If you'd like me to put him out of his misery, just say the word. I have no need of him now that he's cooperated so well."

"What do you want?" I stepped forward.

The soldiers' bows stretched tighter. But Uncle raised his hand to stop them from shooting. Instead, he gave me a cool smile, one that cracked the pockmarked skin of his face. I instead focused on his dark hair, which contrasted with the white hood of his cloak.

"She wants to know what I want." Uncle exchanged a glance with Edgar. "What *do* I want?"

Edgar slid from his mount and crossed toward me. With each footstep, my muscles tightened. When I risked a quick glance next to me, I saw Bulldog's lips had curled in a snarl. I put a steadying hand upon his arm.

Once Sir Edgar stood before me, he flashed a wide smile. Then with a vicious, almost brutal yank, he tore off my cap, ripping strands of hair with it.

I cried out at the pain.

Bulldog lunged for Edgar, but before Bulldog could manage a punch or kick, soldiers surrounded him and dragged him back. They yanked his arms upward behind him so that he had no choice but to fall to his knees with a moan of pain.

My hair tumbled down my shoulders. It was already damp from the rain, but with the steady patter now hitting my head, the curls flattened against my cheeks.

"It's so nice to see you again." Edgar tossed my cap to the ground. "Lady Eleanora."

I didn't respond.

"Or should I say, Cousin?"

"I'm not your cousin."

He grinned again. Then, before I knew what was coming, he raised the back of his hand and smacked me across the mouth, his knuckles making contact with my lips.

The metallic taste of blood oozed between my teeth and onto my tongue.

"No more lies, Juliana." He straightened his shoulders. "Or should I once more correct myself and say, Cloaked Bandit."

I lifted my chin, and a trickle of blood dribbled off and onto my cloak. I met Edgar's smirk head on and didn't flinch.

So this was it. They'd finally caught me.

# Chapter
## 15

I STEPPED LIGHTLY THROUGH THE BRUSH, ATTEMPTING TO cover my tracks. Glancing up, I squinted through the rain into the branches overhead. I expected to see a lookout guard, hear the soft blue jay call the peasants used in warning, or even find Bulldog lying in wait for me like the first time I'd come into the forest. But in the hour since I'd left my horse and men behind, I'd sensed no one.

Even with the light patter of rain on the leaves that were left on the trees, the woodland was too quiet. My gut told me something wasn't right. The peasants always kept watch for intruders entering their deep area of the forest. Where were they today?

I studied the foliage, the trees, and the ground. Someone had been in the woods. And whoever it was hadn't been very careful. I knelt and pushed back a tangle of brambles. There in the mud and sludge of fallen leaves were hoof prints. I shoved aside more of the thicket, revealing the clear outline of large boots.

I straightened, and my heart took a dive into my stomach.

Surely the prints were only those of scouts, the men Lord Wessex had sent in an attempt to find Juliana and her people. The soldiers wouldn't be able to locate the hidden passageway. It was impossible to find without someone guiding them there.

Nevertheless, I lengthened my stride until I was almost running through the forest, heedless now of covering my tracks. My pulse pounded louder until it roared through my head. When I finally crashed through the brush surrounding the wide, old tree that led to the caves, I tried to catch my breath.

But at the sight that met me, fear pierced my chest. Blankets, rags, sleeping pallets, and the few possessions the peasants owned had been strewn over the ground and crushed. In the middle of all the destruction was a body sprawled facedown—a thin boy with a patch of dirty, straw-colored hair poking from beneath a cap.

"Blessed Mary." I bolted toward the body, knelt next to it, and gently rolled him over. "Thatch."

The boy's eyes were closed and his face pale and bruised and beaten. One glance at his broken arms and bloody fingertips gave me all the information I needed to know about what had happened.

Thatch had apparently allowed his anger to make him careless, and had wandered too close to one of Wessex's patrol while running off yesterday. The soldiers had captured the boy, tortured him, and under the duress of pain, Thatch surely told Wessex everything he hadn't already gleaned from William and Mistress Higgins about Juliana and the Cloaked Bandit. Wessex had probably then set the boy free in order to follow him, and, inadvertently, Thatch led the cruel lord directly to the peasants' hiding place.

I pressed my fingers against the pulse in the boy's neck and felt for the rise and fall of his chest.

Thatch's eyelids fluttered open. "Lord Collin," he managed between cracked lips that revealed a gap where he'd obviously lost several more teeth.

I let out a relieved sigh. The boy was still alive.

"I'm sorry," Thatch croaked, closing his eyes. Tears squeezed out and rolled down his temples.

"You had no choice." I brushed my fingertips across the boy's forehead, flicking off the dirt and bits of leaves that had stuck there. "Torture can make even the best man do things he'd never consider under normal circumstances."

Thatch shuddered and pried his eyes open. "You have to go after them. You have to free her."

I nodded. My body had already tensed with the need to fight. My mind had cleared as it did before a battle. I was past ready to charge after Lord Wessex and fight him to the death.

But first, I had to tend to Thatch. And anyone else Wessex had hurt. I scanned the carnage for other bodies.

"The women and children are still hidden underground," Thatch said. "But they took all the men and Juliana as prisoners."

The mere thought of Juliana at Lord Wessex's mercy was too agonizing to imagine. I wanted to hit something, to rage until I was hoarse. I couldn't bear to think what Wessex was planning to do to her.

"Go," Thatch whispered weakly.

"How long have they been gone?

"I can't be sure, but maybe an hour or two."

If I ran fast enough, I might be able to catch up. But what could I do by myself against Wessex and his army of well-trained soldiers? I'd be wiser to approach Wessex calmly and with my own guards accompanying me. I had to stay rational even though my heart was pulsing with the need to rescue Juliana before it was too late, before she ended up like Thatch . . . or worse.

"Go after her and leave me to die," Thatch said more urgently. "After what I did, I don't want to live."

I slid my hands under the boy as carefully as I could, but Thatch cried out in agony nonetheless. I suspected the thumbscrews hadn't worked to get Thatch to cooperate, and so Wessex had resorted to methodically breaking bones in the boy's body.

Fresh anger flooded my chest and poured into my limbs. How could Wessex be so callous to these poor, helpless people?

But even as the question stirred my blood, shame whispered through me. I'd been callous too. Maybe I hadn't been cruel in the same way as Wessex, but I'd been ignorant and uncaring of their plight. I'd lived in luxury without giving any thought to their needs.

And now I prayed it wasn't too late to change.

"I'll go rescue the others," I said. "But first, we need to take care of you and the women and children." Before Thatch could protest again, I lifted him into my arms.

The boy gave another tortured scream, but blessedly fell into unconsciousness.

My hands had grown numb from the lack of blood flowing into my arms. Suspended by chains to the stone wall above my head, my wrists were raw where the metal dug into my skin. My toes barely touched the dungeon floor, even with the soiled straw I'd managed to slide underneath my feet in an effort to relieve the strain on my arms.

My throat burned and my mouth was parched. My face ached in each place Edgar had hit me. And my back was sore from the well-placed kicks he'd given me during the walk back to Wessex.

From the clinking of chains, the soft groans, and the heavy breathing, I knew the others were still alive too. But for how long?

When Uncle had marched us through the gatehouse and into the inner bailey, he'd narrowed his eyes upon me and said, "Welcome home, Lady Juliana. Enjoy being here while you can."

I had no doubt he was planning to put me to death. I just prayed he'd show me mercy and take my life swiftly instead of prolonging the torture.

"Bulldog," I whispered through the dank darkness.

He grunted from the cell across from mine.

"When they come for me, you need to overpower the guards and free yourself and the others."

"I'm not leaving you here to die by yourself."

"You take the others and run as fast as you can to Lord Collin. He'll give you refuge."

A clanking at the entrance of the dungeon sent a burst of urgency through me. "Please, Bulldog. I'll be able to meet my death without fear if I know you and the others are safe."

"If we attempt to overthrow the guards, we'll only end up butchered."

"You'll end up dead anyway."

Before I could argue with him further, the door squealed on its rusty hinges and opened wide. The heavy slap of boots and the brilliance of torchlight filled the dungeon. There were too many guards to count, obviously sent to bring all of us out to receive Uncle's punishment.

My hope fizzled away. When I met Bulldog's gaze, there wasn't a speck of rebellion left in the depths. I had the feeling life had drained out of him when the soldiers had forced him to walk away from Thatch, to leave his only son half dead and sprawled on the ground.

When the guards released my hands from the iron clamps on the wall, I had the brief vision of lashing out at them, of leading an uprising myself. But my arms were so weak and numb from lack of blood that I couldn't make my fingers work. My shoulders and sockets burned from the long hours in one position. I could hardly manage to walk without tripping between the two guards who led me up the winding staircase and out into the courtyard.

I gulped in a breath of the fresh, cold air, knowing it would likely be one of my last. And as the guards marched me through the castle gates and into the town's market square, I lifted my eyes heavenward. Even though the sky was clouded with the ominous gray of more rain, I envisioned my father peering down at me from heaven.

Maybe he wouldn't be proud of everything I'd done, but today, finally, I'd be able to see him again and hug him. At least I could count one blessing from my capture.

When I reached the center green of the marketplace, where my uncle and cousin were waiting, the guards shoved me to my knees in front of them. I lowered my head and let my long, unruly curls hang in my face so that I wouldn't have to look at the two men who'd destroyed my world.

Of course a crowd had gathered for the proceedings. I had no doubt many of them were curious to see me again after believing I'd been dead these past years.

My uncle spoke to the gathering for several minutes, listing my crimes as the Cloaked Bandit.

"What do you have to say for yourself, Lady Juliana?" Uncle's sharp question cut into me. Was he giving me the chance to defend myself? Or was he merely wishing to humiliate me further?

I lifted my head and finally glanced at my uncle and cousin. Though my uncle was attired in pristine white as usual, I could only see the blackness of his heart. It showed through his eyes and the cruel lines in his face.

Next to me, a stake had been erected along with a heap of rain-drenched logs and branches. So they were planning to burn me? I shuddered with a momentary chill at the prospect of slowly roasting to death. The wet wood would drag out the torture for hours.

Uncle bent until his face was mere inches from mine. "I expect that you'll admit to the charges leveled against you, that you will clearly confirm your guilt to this multitude."

"And why would I give you the pleasure of such a confession?" I lifted my chin and glared at him.

Edgar's backhand and knuckles connected with my cheek. Pain erupted in my head, shooting through my face up into my temple. My mind flickered with the edges of blackness. If only he would hit me hard enough to knock me unconscious.

Edgar took a step back and gave me a cool smile. "*My lord*. You forgot to say *my lord*. Don't neglect Lord Wessex's title of respect again."

Uncle cleared his throat. "I would like you to stand and face the crowd, and tell them all that you are indeed guilty of the crimes I have enumerated."

I glanced then to the onlookers who surrounded the market square, the weary and worn faces of tradesmen, villagers, and even peasant farmers who'd assembled to witness my execution. They were strangely somber, their eyes sad, their shoulders stooped. In fact, many of the faces were creased with resentment, eyes slanted with anger.

These people held no love for Uncle. He'd done nothing to earn their respect and trust during the years he'd ruled them. With his high taxes and harsh retribution, he'd instilled nothing in them but fear and hatred.

They surely wouldn't hold my crimes against me. In fact, I'd heard rumors that people admired the Cloaked Bandit for standing up to Lord Wessex.

Even so, they could not stop my death today. They were powerless to do anything against my uncle, not without bringing the same fate upon themselves.

I pressed my lips together. Uncle might be able to kill me, but I wouldn't give him the satisfaction of answering for my crimes.

At a nod from Uncle, the soldier at my side yanked on the chain binding my hands together at my back and dragged me to my feet. I couldn't keep a cry from escaping at the pain that ripped through my arms. The soldier forced me to turn and face the crowd.

Uncle hissed near my ear, "Confess your sins."

"You may as well tie me to the stake first," I murmured.

"I was afraid you'd be stubborn, just like your father." He nodded at the group of soldiers who'd been guarding Bulldog and the other peasant men who'd been captured with me. The soldier grabbed one of the men and shoved him forward, toward a rack-like structure that had been crudely assembled near the stake. It was Jack, who'd been the judge the night of the archery contest. Several soldiers stripped him of his cloak and tunic and then wrestled him backward onto the boards, spreading his hands and feet and tying him down.

"For every minute of your delay," Uncle said, "I shall disembowel one peasant."

One of the soldiers had produced a sharp hook and raised it above Jack's taut stomach, ready to plunge it deep inside and pull out his entrails—another cruel and painful method of killing.

The panic upon Jack's face and the wildness of his eyes grabbed my heart with a panic of my own. "Stop!" I cried out. "Don't hurt him!"

"Very well, Lady Juliana," Uncle said with a nod to the soldier holding the hook. "What have you to say in regard to all the crimes that have been leveled against you?"

Once again I studied the faces of the people who circled the village green. Their hopelessness and wretchedness peered back at me. Suddenly, all I could think was that I'd let them down. I'd failed them. I, Lady Juliana, true master of the lands of Wessex, had failed to protect and provide for *my* people.

I swallowed the growing lump in my throat. What had I ever really done to help them? Sure, I'd provided safety to the most needy. I'd kept them from starving and from perishing in the cold. But none of my efforts had truly brought them the relief and freedom they deserved. My father had been nobler in his attempt to rise up and rebel against his brother. Yes, he'd failed, but at least he'd acted with integrity, and he'd had the courage to attempt something that could benefit our people. In comparison, my efforts seemed so futile and hopeless. If only I'd realized earlier that it never pays to fight evil with evil. But after watching my father die, I'd been consumed with bitterness and had allowed it to lead me astray from what was righteous and pleasing to God.

Now all I could hope for was that Bulldog and the other men would die free of torture, that they would meet their Maker as painlessly as possible.

I straightened my aching shoulders and let the wind bite my bruised cheeks and whip my tangled hair. "My good people, I am guilty of all the crimes of which Lord Wessex has spoken. I have stolen money and jewels. I have destroyed caravans and taken riches that did not belong to me. I have hunted on forbidden lands. And I have poached countless game."

My confession rang out clear and loud across the marketplace. Even the children peering from the open windows of overhanging, two-story shops stared at me with wide, sad eyes.

"Thank you, Lady Juliana," Uncle said with a satisfied smile that crinkled the uneven skin of his face.

I shook off the hand of the soldier holding my arm. "I only regret that I didn't do more to ease your suffering," I called to the crowd, defiance shooting into me. "You have not deserved this cruelty that has befallen you, and I shall breathe my last in the prayer that somehow, someway, God will give you relief from your suffering."

Angry, discontent murmurs rose in the air. From behind, Edgar gave me a shove that sent me stumbling forward, toward the stake.

"You have heard Lady Juliana's guilt," Uncle called out above the growing clamor. "She has confessed with her own lips crimes too numerous to recount."

The soldier wrenched me against the wooden pole.

"And for her crimes," Uncle shouted, "she is hereby sentenced to be burned to death at the stake."

# Chapter
## 16

*The rope bit into my wrists, and slivers from the* stake dug into the tender skin of my arms. The soldiers had made quick work of piling the wet wood around me. Uncle had called in more guards to stand along the edges of the crowd, and had even resorted to beating several men who'd protested too loudly.

Bulldog stood with the others not far away, his stocky head down in defeat. Some of the guards were building a makeshift scaffold.

I had no doubt that while I was slowly roasting to death, my uncle planned to hang each of my companions one by one right before my eyes. At least I could console myself that the men would die quickly, without much pain or humiliation—unlike myself.

A guard approached the stack of wood with a blazing torch. I squared my shoulders and held my chin high. I would face death with dignity and show my uncle that while he could defeat my body, he couldn't defeat my spirit.

"Wait!" came a distant shout.

The soldier carrying the torch stopped and spun in the direction of a group of men riding through the town gates, wearing armor and outfitted with swords.

"Release the prisoners," came a shouted command in a voice that resembled Collin's, only much harsher and fiercer.

My uncle and cousin were now reclining in plush chairs that had been placed in the center of the green, where they were sipping wine and watching the proceedings. At the sight of the company of men, they both stood. Edgar issued a call to their retinue of well-trained soldiers, who immediately raced to surround the newcomers.

I strained to see through the armor and milling of men on horses, their swords raised and ready to fight if needed. One of the knights pushed through the circle of bowmen, knocking them aside as easily as dry wheat stalks. He deflected several arrows with his shield and slashed the hemp string of many more bows, rendering them useless.

When the knight reared his horse and charged in my direction, my heart gave a wild leap. Even though the knight's face was hidden by his helmet, Collin's green eyes sought me from the slit in the visor.

My knees gave way, and I would have slid down the stake had my hands not been tied tightly enough behind me to keep me in place. I didn't know how he'd discovered my capture; all I cared about was that he was there.

If anyone could save me and my companions, surely Lord Collin Goodrich could.

"Release Lady Juliana this instant," he yelled, cutting down another of Uncle's soldiers who came at him.

Uncle and Edgar exchanged glances, almost as if they'd been expecting Collin.

"Good evening to you too, Lord Collin," called Uncle. "It's nice to see you again after your unexplained absence."

Collin sidled his steed near them. "You've overstepped your bounds. You've arrested and taken into captivity innocent people."

Uncle's brow shot up. "Innocent? I hardly think one can call Lady Juliana innocent."

"She's done nothing but help the hungry and impoverished who have suffered as a result of your harsh hand. If she's guilty of any wrongdoing, then surely you and I are even more so because of our callousness."

"She very well could have brought her complaints before us in a peaceful way," Edgar said, then took a sip from his goblet. "Instead, she resorted to stealing."

"Have you not stolen this land and this estate from her?" Collin countered. "And have you not stolen from the people when you demand more taxes of them than they can pay?"

I wanted to shout my agreement, but at the arrival of more armed Wessex soldiers on the outskirts of the crowd, I realized Uncle was well-prepared for any objections to the public execution. His small army would soon surround and outnumber Collin and his men.

"This estate is rightfully mine. I have a letter from my father that proves it." Uncle pushed back the white hood of his cloak to reveal his scarred face. "Besides, my brother is dead. And now Lady Juliana is a criminal and unfit to lead."

"In your opinion, she's unfit merely because she's alive and poses a threat to your rule." Collin's tone was as unyielding as his armor.

Edgar's lips curved into a half smile, one I'd learned only masked his anger. "You're too bold, Lord Collin. You'd be wise to return to your land and let us handle our own problems without interference."

"You made it my problem when your sheriff unlawfully took two of my most loyal servants."

My stomach swirled with fresh revulsion. I didn't have to deliberate long to figure out which servants Uncle had taken to glean information about me. Mistress Higgins and William were the only two with whom I'd had any significant contact.

"What other choice did you give us when you were deliberately shielding a criminal who has been perpetrating violence and civil disobedience upon our land?" Uncle surveyed the perimeter of the village square. Collin did likewise.

Uncle had always had a strong army, and now they stood in formation, ready for combat. Collin was certainly in no position—no matter how experienced he was—to take on the army with his small band of soldiers.

But if Uncle's army unnerved Collin, he didn't show it. "Let Lady Juliana go," he demanded. "Now."

"I will release your two servants, but you have no claim over Lady Juliana."

Collin's fingers flexed on the hilt of his sword. He shifted in his saddle, his body taut, almost as if he longed to start a battle at that moment. But when his gaze connected again with mine over the piles of logs surrounding me, there was a desperation in his eyes that belied his strength.

Would he be unable to secure my release after all? My heart quivered. Part of me demanded that I accept the consequences of stealing and breaking the law. I'd known it was wrong, but I'd tossed aside the niggling guilt and told myself that whatever I did couldn't compare with the atrocities Uncle had committed.

But the other part of me yearned to be set free. Even though I'd lived recklessly and dangerously, I wasn't ready to die yet. Not until I had the chance to do more to truly set my people free, this time the right way.

"She has committed many crimes," Uncle said. "And if I don't punish her, I will only send the message to my people that they too can perpetuate transgressions and go unpunished. Such a stance is surely the forerunner to facilitating more depravity and sin."

"You will send the message of mercy and kindness," Collins retorted.

Edgar gave a scoffing laugh, and Uncle narrowed his eyes. "Sometimes leaders must execute judgment that serves a purpose for the greater good of everyone."

"For the greater good of *you*." Collin's words throughout his confrontation had drawn nods and murmurs of assent from the gathering. "Only you stand to gain anything by Lady Juliana's death."

"Enough!" Uncle's voice rose above the din of the crowd. "She has been sentenced to die, and there's nothing you or anyone else can do to change that."

"You don't have any evidence against her, just the words of my two servants and a helpless young peasant boy. And that's not enough to condemn her to death."

"Ah, but that is where you are wrong, Lord Collin." Uncle's lips curved into a tight smile. "This entire assembly has witnessed Lady Juliana confess her offenses with her own lips. She has readily admitted to the long list of grievances against herself."

I gave an inward groan. I'd played into Uncle's hands, had done exactly as he'd hoped. And now that I'd confessed to the crimes, I surely must pay. What other choice did I have?

Collin was silent as if recognizing the futility of negotiating any further with my uncle. The only way he could free me was by brute force, and if he attempted anything, he would be overpowered and cut down swiftly.

Uncle motioned to the soldier holding the torch, and the young man turned back to the wet wood that surrounded me. Defeat swept over me. If only I'd stayed the course my father had set out for me. If only I'd refused to lower myself into a lifestyle of sinfulness and stealing.

"If someone must pay for Lady Juliana's crimes," Collin called out, his voice tinged with panic. "Then I give you myself."

My head shot up.

The torchbearer once again hesitated in front of the wood, turning to Uncle for his instructions.

"I will die in her place," Collin called.

"No," I said quickly. "I'm guilty. I'm the one who deserves death. Not you."

"If you release her"—Collin stared pointedly at Uncle, clearly ignoring me—"then I will allow you to bind my hands and tie me to the stake in her place."

"No!" I cried. But the gasps and shouts from the crowd drowned out my protests.

Uncle and Edgar exchanged glances as they'd done before. And something about Edgar's sneer sent alarm bells clanging in my soul.

"And you must release the peasant men, along with my two servants," Collin added. "If you set them free with Lady Juliana, I will hand myself over to you without raising a hand to defend myself."

The clamors of surprise among the crowd had grown louder.

Across the distance, among the peasants awaiting their hanging, Bulldog had lifted his head, and for the first time since we'd arrived at the castle something sparked in his eyes.

When his fierce gaze met mine, I knew he would support Collin's plan, that he would be of no help in stopping Collin from taking my place. I shook my head at Bulldog, hoping he would see my eyes pleading to put an end to the foolishness.

But he only pursed his lips in silence. He would say nothing. His eyes said it all—he was determined to free me, and he didn't care if Collin had to die for that to happen.

Uncle and Sir Edgar argued in hushed tones for several long moments before Uncle finally lifted his hand for attention. Slowly, silence descended over the crowd.

"Very well, Lord Collin," Uncle said with a satisfied smile wrinkling his cheeks. "If you're willing to give up your life for

Lady Juliana's, then we shall count that as full payment for her crimes."

"And those of her friends," Collin demanded, nodding at Bulldog and the others.

"Yes," Uncle replied. "We shall set them all free, as long as they agree to move off Wessex and never step foot on my land again. If they ever return, I shall consider them in breach of our agreement and shall kill them on the spot."

"Take her to my land, to my home," Collin called to Bulldog. "You'll find refuge there."

Bulldog gave a curt nod. But everything within me rose up in protest. I wanted to scream, but my lungs pinched. Collin's action would not only save me—he was offering me a way to save all my friends. His one life for many. How could I argue with that?

"If you throw down your weapons," Uncle said to Collin, "then I shall start releasing the peasants."

For a moment, Collin conversed with his men, his voice rising in clear disagreement with theirs. Finally, amidst their protest, he dropped his sword, then he threw down his knives along with his bow and arrows.

Even though I couldn't argue against saving the lives of my many friends, my chest constricted with anguish. I wouldn't let him sacrifice himself for me. The truth was, I didn't want to lose him. I didn't want him to die. Not for me. Not for anyone.

"Let my companions go," I cried, "but keep me! I won't let Lord Collin take my place."

Collin reared on his steed again, letting the horse raise its hooves high in the air and push back the soldiers that had been crouching closer to him. "I must see Lady Juliana and these peasant men released safely outside the town gates before I dismount."

Already one of the soldiers had begun to twist at the knot binding my wrists. Within seconds he'd freed my hands and legs from the confines of the stake. I stumbled through the wood pile and collapsed to my knees. I didn't care that tears were streaking my cheeks or that I was begging.

"Please! I'm the only one who deserves death. Let the others go."

But Bulldog had also been loosened from his binding, and he charged toward me. He grabbed my arm and forced me back to my feet. "Let's go. Now."

I tried to wrench free of his grip, but he jerked me forward. I struggled against him until finally, with a low snarl, he grabbed me and hefted me so that I dangled over his shoulder. The crowd of townspeople had parted to allow us to escape. The other peasant men raced forward, casting anxious glances over their shoulders as though expecting Uncle's soldiers to chase after them and lock them back up.

Bulldog trotted after our companions, his grip like iron, unrelenting in his determination to put as much distance between me and my uncle as he could. Silent sobs choked me. I could hear Collin ordering his men to escort us to his land and to keep us safe there. When I lifted my head and swiped aside a tangle of curls, I sought out Collin. A sad good-bye radiated from his eyes . . . and something else I couldn't quite define.

Then, while he was caught off guard watching me, one of Uncle's guards swung a pike against Collin's head. The force of the blow knocked him backward. In an instant, he fell from his horse into the thick of the guards, who lashed out at him with vicious kicks and punches.

Their shouts and cheers tore at my heart. I thrashed against Bulldog, knowing I had to go back and help Collin. But my friend wouldn't release me, and all I could do was weep with an agony I'd never known before.

# Chapter

## 17

*I knelt in the damp leaves, my head bowed low and* cradled in my hands. Gratefully, the others had left me alone in my misery. And now the darkness of the night shielded me from their prying eyes.

The men were too busy rejoicing at being reunited with their wives and children. And they were eating from among the provisions Collin's servants had brought out to them after we'd arrived on Goodrich land several hours ago.

"O Father in heaven, forgive my trespasses," I whispered, rocking back and forth. My eyes burned, my throat ached, and my entire body keened with such longing, I wanted to cry. Except that I'd already shed all the tears I could, and now I had none left. I'd prayed all the prayers I knew, and now I could only kneel before God, speechless, broken, and empty.

The soft laughter of the families gathered around blazing fires beckoned me to return to the camp. But the sight of the mound of warm blankets, the piles of fresh food, and the assortment of supplies they would need to start new lives only mocked me.

And reminded me of Collin and the wonderful man he truly was.

Although Collin's men had left him reluctantly, each one had obeyed his orders to escort us. They'd accompanied us to our cave homes, helped us retrieve the women and children and any supplies we could salvage, and then had delivered us safely to the forests of Goodrich land.

Not only that, they'd brought wagonload after wagonload of supplies to us, according to the direction Collin had given them before his capture. Collin had assured our well-being and had obviously been planning all along to bring us to safety upon his land.

"Oh, Collin," I said. "I'm so sorry."

How could I have ever believed him to be mean and uncaring? I'd been wrong to lump all noblemen together in the same category as Uncle. I'd wanted to blame someone for all the heartache that had befallen me and my father, and it had been all too easy to point the finger at the nobility.

But Collin had proven that the problems didn't belong to one class of people. He'd shown himself to be a good and decent man—not perfect, but certainly willing to learn and change. He'd shown that nobility could use their power to bring about good for the people just as easily as the nobility could use their power to crush and destroy.

And now he was dead because of me.

I rocked back and forth again, my head pounding with the horror of what he'd had to endure on account of me: the hours of slow roasting, of tortured agony. I wanted to die at just the thought of it.

A thumbless hand upon my back halted my inner torment for a moment. "Juliana," Bulldog whispered. "Come and eat."

He hadn't joined the others either. He'd sat apart from them, watching me.

I knew he was still grieving over Thatch. We hadn't found a trace of the boy when we'd searched the land surrounding our homes. Bulldog had finally given up hope of finding the body. I'd known, as he had, that some wild animal had likely dragged the lifeless body away into the depths of the forest.

"You need to have something," Bulldog said gently, patting my back awkwardly in an unusual show of affection.

"I'm not hungry."

He sighed, the breath long and weary. For a moment, he stood behind me. Then his hand fell away from my back, and the crunching of his footsteps told me he'd gone back to his lonely spot.

Part of me longed to go to him, to offer him comfort, which he needed just as much as I did. I ought to reassure him I wasn't angry with him for dragging me away from Collin. He'd done the right thing, even if I'd resented it at the time.

The truth was, there was nothing any of us could have done to save Collin.

"O Father in heaven," I cried into my hands again. My heart wrenched with the awfulness of all that had happened. And losing Collin was the worst part.

I finally had to admit—although I hadn't known him long, it had been long enough to know he was the kind of man I could have loved.

And now I'd lost him.

My chest tightened. Even more painful than the knowledge that I'd missed out on loving him was the realization that he'd sacrificed his life for me . . . even though he'd believed I held no love for him. He'd given up his life for me in spite of the fact that I'd rejected him, his love, and his proposal of marriage. He'd willingly taken my place at the stake even though I'd sent him away.

A sob rose from deep inside me. I'd been a fool to spurn him.

And now I'd never have the chance to admit to him what I'd been denying—that I was falling for him, that I wanted the chance to make things work between us . . .

I sucked in a deep breath of the cold night air. The frigidness penetrated my lungs and mind.

What if I attempted to atone for my past mistakes by fighting against Uncle the right way? What if I rallied the people throughout Wessex to rise up in revolt as my father had done? Maybe my father hadn't been able to defeat Uncle through his rebellion, but at least he'd taken a stand against the cruelty.

The people were ready. I'd seen it in their faces earlier when they'd gathered to watch the executions.

A call from the camp broke into my thoughts. I sat up and wiped my dirty hands across my eyes. There, on the fringe of the gathering, outlined in the glow of the firelight, was one of Collin's soldiers. He slid from his mount and glanced around, obviously searching for someone.

"Lady Juliana?" he called.

At the note of urgency in his voice, I pushed myself off the ground and moved from the dark shadows of the woodland into the reaches of the firelight.

"I am Lady Juliana," I said, speaking the title I'd loathed for so many years. It was time to finally acknowledge what I'd tried to ignore, tried to destroy. The fact was, no amount of disguise and no amount of denial could change who I was, the person I was born to be.

"Lady Juliana." The soldier bowed toward me. Then upon straightening, he nodded at Bulldog, who'd taken his place at my side.

"What tidings do you bring?" I asked, noticing then that the soldier was breathing just as hard as his mount. He'd obviously made haste to find me.

"I have both good news and bad," he blurted.

"Do not spare me," I ordered. "Tell me everything you know."

"The good news is that Lord Collin is still alive."

My knees turned as weak as a willow branch. I would have collapsed had Bulldog not snaked his arm around my waist and held me up.

"Thanks be to God," I whispered, tears stinging my eyes. I swallowed hard, pushing down a sudden relieved sob. Instead, I forced myself to rise to the leadership role that this soldier expected. "For how long has his life been spared?"

"We've just received the missive that Lord Collin is to be drawn, hung, and quartered in two days' time."

"Two days." The words sent a charge of energy through me. "Two days isn't long, but it's better than none."

"Don't even start thinking of trying to stop Lord Wessex," Bulldog groused.

I pulled away from my friend. "How can I do anything less? I'll find a way to rally the people to rise up and fight."

Bulldog shook his head. "You heard the lord. He'll kill anyone who steps a foot back into Wessex."

"We'll arm the townspeople and everyone throughout the countryside," I continued, ignoring my friend's scowl and the silence of the others. "If we rise together, we can fight against my uncle and put an end to his brutal reign."

"You'll only face the same fate as your father." Bulldog spat the words.

"Then at least I'll have done something noble for once in my life."

My impassioned words silenced him. Collin's soldier watched me, admiration lighting his face. I would call upon Collin's men to help too. Surely with their training and weapons, we could work together to bring down Uncle.

"And what of the bad news?" I asked, my mind already at work, the weariness suddenly gone.

"Lord Edgar has claimed Lady Irene as his betrothed," the soldier replied. "They are to be married immediately after Lord Collin's execution."

The news brought a deathly silence over the camp.

Upon Collin's death, Lady Irene would inherit the vast Goodrich estate. And through the marriage, my cousin Edgar would become master of the Goodrich land and wealth. That meant none of us would be able to take refuge on Goodrich land. The supplies Collin had arranged for us would be cut off. And if Edgar had persecuted us before, surely he would resume.

At the somber expressions of my men, I knew they'd come to the same conclusion.

An unsettled thought came to me. Had Uncle used me as bait to draw Collin into his grip? Had he realized that if he captured me, he could control Collin? After all, what did it matter if I died? I had nothing. But Uncle stood to gain so much more if Collin were eliminated.

I straightened my shoulders, not caring that my tangled hair hung about my face in a wild disarray. "The news of the betrothal is all the more reason to rise against Lord Wessex."

Bulldog grunted, but I was relieved when he didn't voice any further protest. I needed his support. The men were much more likely to follow me if Bulldog was at my side, leading the way with me.

The clatter of branches and leaves signaled the approach of another rider. This time as the horse broke through the foliage into the clearing where we'd set up camp, Bulldog pulled his knife and the other men followed suit.

We were no longer safe, and we all knew it.

At the sight of the Goodrich coat of arms upon the new arrival's armor, the tension eased from my muscles. Through the darkness, I could see the outline of a boy on the horse behind the soldier.

Bulldog started. "Lord God Almighty be praised," he whispered in a voice thick with emotion. Then he bolted forward, throwing himself at the boy.

My heart sped in recognition too. "Thatch?"

A head peeked from behind the soldier, the wiry hair standing on end and poking out in every direction.

A lump lodged in my throat. When Bulldog eased the boy off the horse and gently lifted him into his arms, I wanted to sink to my knees in relief.

Bulldog kissed his son's forehead. Tears streamed down the hardened man's face, falling onto the boy.

"I'm sorry, Dad," Thatch croaked, his own tears making trails down his bruised cheeks. "I never meant to betray everyone—"

"Hush now, boy." Bulldog carried him as tenderly as a baby. "Don't say anything more about it. We're all safer now than we've been in a long time."

I didn't contradict him. Now wasn't the time.

Thatch strained his head, glancing around the camp in search of someone. "Juliana?"

I swiped at my cheeks and then stepped further into the firelight where he could see me. "I'm here."

Bulldog swerved toward me.

The boy's eyes again flooded with tears. He started to reach a hand out to me, but stopped. Someone had bandaged his arms and hands in clean cloths and tended his wounds, but even so, the grimace on his face indicated the pain the movement brought him.

"Juliana," he whispered as Bulldog brought him closer—close enough that I could see the bend in his nose where it had been broken. "Can you ever forgive me?"

"This isn't your fault." I laid a gentle hand upon his bandaged one. "My uncle was bound to find us sooner or later. We couldn't go on the way we were forever." I spoke the words more to Bulldog than Thatch.

"But if I hadn't run off and been so reckless—"

"I've always been the reckless one and haven't set a good example for you. And I'm deeply sorry for that now."

They boy's eyes reflected a sadness and maturity that hadn't been there before. "I was wrong about Collin."

"Say no more," Bulldog said, starting away from me toward the blankets.

"Wait!" Thatch protested. "He rescued me. He brought me back to his home and cared for me even though he was anxious to rescue Juliana."

Bulldog stopped.

"He's a better man than most," Thatch spoke passionately. "If not for him, I'd be dead."

The light and shadows from the fire flickered across Bulldog's face, revealing both his fierceness and vulnerability at the same time. Thatch didn't say anything more. He closed his eyes, weariness making his features sag.

I worked with Bulldog to make a bed out for Thatch of the blankets. We made him as comfortable as possible before sitting back on our heels.

"We have to try to rescue Collin," I said.

Bulldog shook his head and stared straight ahead at the flames. "We can't put everyone at risk for one man."

"But he saved me." I didn't care that I was pleading. "And he saved Thatch."

Bulldog gazed at the boy, his eyes radiating with relief and love.

"It's time to finish what my father started," I said, knowing deep in my heart that was what he would have wanted. Even if I died in the process, we needed to stand up to my uncle once and for all. "We have to stop hiding away. And we have to stop blaming the wealthy for all the problems. Our tactics haven't been fair."

Bulldog smoothed his thick fingers across Thatch's peaceful, sleeping face. "If we cross over into Wessex, we won't return alive."

I merely nodded. Uncle had ensured Collin's death by forbidding us from coming back onto Wessex land. He'd thought to keep us from attempting a rescue. But my uncle obviously didn't know me well enough to realize I'd do what I wanted regardless of his bargain with Collin.

Whether Bulldog came with me or not, I was going back. "I'm ready to die."

"I'm not sure that I'm ready to let you." His voice was a desperate whisper.

"You've fulfilled your promise to my father. You've kept me safe. You've brought me to adulthood." I reached for his maimed hand and squeezed it between mine. "But now it's my turn to do what's right. To stand up against Uncle. And to sacrifice my life so that no one else has to suffer like Thatch."

Bulldog's fingers tightened around mine as if he didn't want to let me go.

"Don't you want more for Thatch? Don't you want him to have a better life?"

Bulldog didn't respond.

I pulled away from him and stood. I tugged up the hood of my cloak and then checked to make sure knives were strapped at my waist. "I'm leaving. Now. And I'm riding throughout Wessex to rally the people behind me. I'd be honored if you'd ride with me."

He stared at the fire, the muscles in his jaw flexing.

I spun and stalked toward Collin's men, who were still waiting on the fringe of our camp. My heart banged with each step I took away from Bulldog. I wanted his help, but I would fight my uncle and rescue Collin regardless.

A menacing rumble from behind me brought my footsteps to a halt.

"I'm eating first before we leave."

I smiled, and relief blew through me. But I wiped the smile off my face and tossed Bulldog a glare that was mingled with all my affection. "You better hurry up."

He grunted.

"We have two long days ahead of us."

# Chapter
## 18

MY BACK WAS SCRAPED RAW, MY FLESH OPEN AND BLEEDing. The tendons in my legs were stretched beyond endurance, the skin of my ankles rubbed off where the ropes had bound me, and my head felt like it would explode.

I was conscious only because I'd strained to keep my head from bumping the rocks and cobblestones as the horse had galloped through town, dragging me behind by my legs with my body bumping along behind.

And now, at the center green, I blinked away the threatening blackness.

I was already weak from hunger and lack of water from my two days in the dungeon. Lord Wessex had offered me nothing but the tip of his guards' boots. Every time they'd come to check on me, they'd kicked me senseless.

My swollen tongue stuck to the roof of my mouth. And as one of the guards kicked me again, I didn't have the strength to even moan.

"Get to your feet," came the harsh command.

I rolled over and struggled to push myself up. Every muscle and bone in my body screamed. Out of the corner of my eye, I could see the scaffolding where I was to be hung.

Of course, I'd hang until I was almost dead. They wouldn't kill me completely. Wessex would want me alive when they began to slice my body into four pieces for the quartering part of the death sentence.

They would make my death as painful as possible. But I'd much rather be the one suffering than Juliana. Even after two days, I still went cold every time I pictured her tied to the stake with the wood piled around her.

If I'd delayed even an hour longer . . .

I couldn't bear to think about it. All that mattered was that she was safe. She'd live securely on Goodrich land. I'd made sure my most loyal soldiers knew to protect her and her people and to provide them with everything they needed.

"Make haste." The nearest guard booted me in the side, and I couldn't hold back a groan of agony. I had no doubt each of my ribs was already cracked or broken. Nevertheless, I forced myself to my knees and then to my feet, which was difficult without the use of my bound hands.

When I was finally standing, the soldier shoved me roughly toward the scaffolding. I stumbled and almost fell back to my knees.

"Wait," came Wessex's voice from the center of the marketplace. "Perhaps Lord Collin would like to say his final good-byes to his sister."

My sister?

I lifted my head and glanced in the direction where Lord Wessex and Edgar were sitting to watch the execution, the same place they'd been reclining the day I'd ridden into town to free Juliana.

There, next to Edgar in a third smaller but no less ornate chair, sat Irene. She was attired in the most elegant white gown, with lace and pearls embroidered into every inch. Her hair flowed long and loose beneath a veil and was adorned with a wreath of white roses and baby's breath. She was beautiful—almost as beautiful as a bride on her wedding day.

My pulse careened to a stop. Was she getting married? To Edgar?

Across the distance, Irene met my gaze. Her eyes, so much like mine, were wide with horror and reflected the anguish in her soul. More than that, they pleaded with me for forgiveness. Her face was translucent, and the muscles in her long, elegant neck were taut. She sat stiffly and her fingers gripped the arms of her chair, turning her knuckles white.

"Say your good-bye," Edgar ordered her with a half grin. "That's what you wanted, wasn't it?"

She visibly swallowed, and her eyes pleaded with me again for forgiveness.

I nodded at her. She may have been resentful of me for inheriting our father's estate. She may have been cross with me over my initial irresponsibility and carelessness in handling the wealth—and rightly so. And she may have been angry and spiteful with me for telling her no to her choice of a spouse. The truth was, I should have been more sensitive to her all along and perhaps even allowed her to retain some control. Whatever the case, she would never wish me this kind of death.

Even if she'd inadvertently had a role in disclosing Juliana's identity to Wessex, I knew she'd never meant for all this to happen. She was conniving at times, but she wasn't malicious.

Edgar's smile disappeared, and he grabbed Irene's arm hard enough that she winced. "Tell him good-bye so that we can put him to death and get on with the wedding."

So, she *was* getting married to Edgar. My head spun with a vortex of dizziness that threatened more blackness, so that Irene's distressed and impassioned good-bye was like a distant, muted event.

From the gleam of victory in Sir Edgar's eyes, I should have known the rogue had planned my execution with the intention of marrying Irene, and by so doing gain my land and wealth.

A fresh burst of anger and strength rippled through me. No wonder Lord Wessex had been all too willing to let Juliana go. Once Edgar became master of Goodrich, they would hunt the peasants again and treat them as brutally as they always had.

The soldier prodded me up the ladder with the sharp tip of his sword. When I reached the top and straightened to my full height, I glanced around for the first time. The market-place wasn't as crowded as the day Lady Juliana had been brought to the stake. In fact, the gathering was rather sparse, mostly Wessex's soldiers and a few tradesmen and their wives who looked on with faces as blanched as Irene's.

At least I could take comfort in the fact that the people of Wessex had not shown their lord any support for my execution. And I could also take comfort in the fact that Juliana was alive, that she and Bulldog would find a way to escape and survive again as they had before.

The soldier shoved me from behind, sending me stumbling toward the loop of rope that would strangle the breath of life from me, choke my vocal chords, and bring me to the brink of death.

I didn't fight as I was forced to stand upon a stool and shove my head through the noose. When the coarse hemp tightened against my throat, I simply closed my eyes. I was ready to die. I'd prayed enough over the past two days and had made my peace with God. I knew I'd done the only thing I could have by taking Juliana's place.

I loved her more than my own life. Even if she didn't love me in return the same way, I could do nothing less than die for her. I wouldn't have been able to stand back and watch her lose her life, not without dying myself on the inside.

At a command from Wessex, the soldier kicked at the stool and it slipped away, first from one foot and then from the other, so that suddenly the rope bit painfully into my neck. As the pressure of my body pulled down against it, the noose drew tighter.

I dangled in midair, nothing under my feet, my body swaying slightly.

The rope dragged against my chin and cinched against my vocal chords. But I held my eyes closed, willing myself to remain calm even as my throat burned and my airways began to constrict with the lack of air.

Fifteen seconds passed in what seemed an eternity. My legs began to twitch from the lack of oxygen. And my head roared with the growing need to draw a breath.

After another fifteen seconds, I couldn't keep myself from thrashing, the need for air overpowering all of my other senses and reserves.

They would keep me up for at least another minute before cutting me down, although it would be more merciful if they let me die here and spared me the torture of slicing my body open.

When the sharp twang of an arrow rent the air and pierced the rope above my head, I opened my eyes in surprise. The arrow sliced the cord in one swift motion, plummeting me to the scaffold and onto my backside with a hard jolt. Another arrow rapidly followed the first, and this one hit its target— the palm of the soldier who'd been standing guard. The arrow's trajectory and force had also pinned the man's hand to the beam behind me, making him cry out in pain.

Several more arrows hit the soldiers surrounding the scaffold before any of them could react.

I gasped, trying to suck in air. I grappled with the rope, desperate to loosen it so that air could reach my lungs. One look at the clean cut of the twine and I knew what was happening. A sick dread stampeded through my already roiling stomach.

Juliana was there somewhere. No one else but her could hit a target like that—except me.

With panic replacing the burning agony in my throat, I wrenched the noose, prying it free. At the same time, the noon air was split with piercing, warlike cries. The onlookers screamed and began running.

I tossed off the rope and dragged in a deep breath. And then I pulled myself to my feet. A sweeping glance at the perimeter of the town green gave me all the information I needed to know. The peasants of Wessex had risen up in revolt against their lord. They surrounded the marketplace, their crude weapons drawn, their rag clothes their only armor, their faces fierce with determination.

There, at the center of the small army, stood Juliana. Her cheeks were smudged with dirt, her hair pulled back under her men's cap, her garments stained with dried blood and caked with mud. Even so, nothing could hide her beauty, the graceful curve of her chin, the stunning brown of her eyes.

She was achingly beautiful. But she was also stubbornly foolish.

I wanted to march over to her, grab her by the arms, and shake some sense into her. She shouldn't have come back. Didn't she know how slim her chances of defeating Wessex were? Most of the peasants held pitchforks, clubs, and hammers. Only a few had knives or bows. With such a pitiful army, by the day's end she would end up tortured and dead—just like her father?

Yet here she was, at the very center of an uprising. Her bow was taut and her arrows flew as fast as she could draw them. Bulldog stood at her side, his bow working just as swiftly. One glance at Bulldog's face and I knew that he would die first before letting anything happen to Juliana.

Even though I was tempted to rush over and drag her out of the danger, deep inside I realized that the best way to save her was to win the battle against Lord Wessex.

Lord Wessex's soldiers were running every which way, the initial surprise attack and the arrows throwing them into confusion. But my battle training told me they wouldn't be running for long. They'd pull themselves together, and their superior strength and weapons would eventually squelch the peasants.

Unless . . .

I quickly calculated how many swords and lances I could gather from the soldiers Juliana and Bulldog had already wounded. If I could rally the peasants to charge at the soldiers right now, while we still had the element of surprise, we could disarm them and accumulate even more weapons.

Even though my battered body protested each movement I made, I bounded across the scaffold, swiping up the swords of the fallen guards. I swiftly cut my hands free. Then with a deftness born of desperation, I jumped from the scaffold into the screaming fray of people milling in every direction. With the chaos erupting around the scaffold, no one was paying attention to me anymore, and I easily wound through the melee, collecting weapons until my arms ached and my back bent under the weight.

I dumped the weapons on the ground near the fringes of peasant men, who rapidly descended upon the pile. Then with a sword in both hands, I charged forward toward Lord Wessex's men, calling the men to fall into step behind me.

Out of the corner of my eye, I saw archers positioning themselves on the town walls. Once their arrows began to fly, we would begin to suffer casualties. Moreover, we wouldn't have much time until more of Wessex's well-trained guards stationed at the castle heard the commotion and came charging into the battle.

If we could cut down the soldiers already at the square and take even more weapons, then we might possibly stand a chance against the bulk of the army.

With a roar, I swung the swords, deflecting blows while at the same time disarming more soldiers. "Grab as many of their weapons as you can," I shouted over the clank of metal and the fierce cries of those fighting.

An arrow slashed the air near my head. Another quickly followed and plunged into the back of the peasant next to me, who crumpled to the ground with a cry of agony.

I glanced over my shoulder to the town wall, and ducked just in time to avoid the arrow that would have embedded itself into my head. If only I had my bow and arrow, I'd take the archers out one by one. As it was, I was helpless under their onslaught.

An archer pulled back his bow to shoot at me again. Apparently, they were aiming primarily at me. How could I lead the peasants in battle if I had a target on my back? And yet how could I take out the archers before they killed me?

A bowman nearest to me was perched on the walkway of the town wall, his arrow pointed directly at my heart.

Suddenly, an arrow pierced the man's neck in the tiny sliver of exposed skin between his helmet and his chest piece. He stiffened and then toppled forward over the stone wall. I watched as he crashed to the ground, motionless, his bow and quiver of arrows next to him.

A second arrow met the mark in the neck of another archer, then another. I glanced in the direction of Juliana. She had her bow aimed at the wall, at the archers, and was taking them out one by one, her hands flying methodically but faster than any archer I'd ever seen.

I breathed a silent prayer that she'd have enough arrows to stay safe, and then spun back into the onslaught before me, rejoining the peasants in their attack on Lord Wessex's soldiers. My mind, my muscles, and my body went into the focused solider mode that the Duke of Rivenshire had drilled into me. All my aches and pains, my anxiety over Juliana, my doubts about defeating Wessex—everything fell away. I thought of nothing but swinging my swords and cutting down the enemy in order to get more weapons into the hands of the peasants that surrounded me.

I shouted and pushed forward and led the way into the fray, pushing the soldiers back until they retreated down the cobbled street that led back to the castle. I began to relentlessly pursue, when suddenly an eerie silence descended over the market square behind me. The peasants fighting alongside me stopped and turned, their swords hanging useless at their sides.

For several moments I slashed forward, pushing onward, my breath coming in heavy gasps, blood roaring in my ears.

"Drop your weapon, Lord Collin," came Lord Wessex's sharp shout behind me. "Or I'll kill Lady Juliana right here and now."

I spun and lifted my swords, ready to plunge them into Wessex's heart. But at the sight that met me, every ounce of fight drained from my body, leaving me weak and shaking.

"Blessed Mary," I whispered.

There, in the center of the green at the top of the abandoned scaffolding, Edgar had captured Juliana. Her bow and arrow lay trampled at his feet. He'd wrenched her arms behind her back. Her cap was off, and he'd gripped a fistful of her hair and yanked her head back, exposing her neck. In his other hand, he pressed the sharp blade of a knife against her skin hard enough to draw blood.

# Chapter
## 19

"LAY DOWN YOUR WEAPONS," LORD WESSEX DEMANDED again from the foot of the scaffolding. The man's chest heaved in and out. He was sweating profusely. And bright crimson stained the white sleeve of his tunic where the broken shaft of an arrow stuck out.

How had Edgar gotten his hands upon Juliana?

A glance in the direction of where she'd been shooting only moments ago revealed Bulldog sprawled on the ground, unmoving, a pool of blood forming in the dirt at his side.

My gaze swung back to Juliana. Across the distance, her eyes pleaded with me to keep fighting. We had the upper hand. We were doing the unbelievable. We were driving Lord Wessex's army back. We couldn't give up yet. Not now. Not for her.

"Throw down your swords," Wessex called to me, clutching the wound in his arm.

My chest burned and my parched mouth cried out for relief. The inaction made me acutely aware of the flesh wounds in my back from being dragged through town, the ache in my ribs from the endless kicks in the dungeon, and the pain in my neck from where the noose had strangled me.

But none of my pains compared to the agony of seeing Juliana at the mercy of Edgar. The pain was nearly as intense as the agony I'd felt earlier in the week when I'd witnessed her tied to the stake.

"Don't stop!" she cried out. "Fight to the death!"

Edgar yanked her head, pulling her hair hard enough to bring tears to her eyes.

I stepped forward, my body stiffening and my fingers tightening around my swords. Her big brown eyes pleaded with me to keep fighting, to defeat Lord Wessex once and for all—even if she had to die in the process.

The truth in her eyes hit me hard. If I gave up my sword and stopped fighting, Lord Wessex would kill us all anyway. He'd burn Juliana at the stake as he'd initially planned and then finish quartering me. But if I rallied the men to press onward, to ignore Wessex and Edgar—and Juliana—then we still had a chance to win.

As when she was tied at the stake, she wanted me to let her die. She was willing to sacrifice her life so that her people could regain the freedom they desperately needed.

The awfulness of the situation barreled into me, knocking the breath from my lungs. How could I possibly stand back and let Sir Edgar slit her throat? I couldn't.

Again, her eyes pleaded with me to stop standing there, to resume the fight before Wessex's men could regroup and surround us. But I couldn't move. I loved her too much to stand back and watch her die. She had to know that. Even if she didn't love me in return, I'd never stop loving her.

She lowered her lashes, as if she couldn't bear to see the love in my eyes.

I fought against the urge to drop my sword. I knew in the end that her sacrifice, her death, would bring about greater freedom for the peasants she loved and it would put an end to Wessex's tyranny. I could grant her last wish, couldn't I? I could defeat Wessex for her sake, in honor of her.

The renewed yells of Lord Wessex's soldiers echoed in the street behind me. They were rallying to turn the tide of the battle.

Juliana lifted her lashes then and met my gaze one last time. "Please," she mouthed even as she strained away from the sharp blade at her neck.

I gave the barest of nods, the motion wrenching my heart into two.

The resignation within his eyes tore at me. But relief weakened my knees.

My death wouldn't be in vain. Collin would lead the peasants to victory. I'd seen the determination etched in his face from the moment he'd spotted me in the crowd. He'd fought valiantly and pushed the peasant men to do more than I'd dreamed possible.

He'd been wise to go for the weapons first. And his training and experience as a warrior would lead them to victory.

Without me.

I watched him raise his sword above his head, the valor and determination returning. He shouted to the men surrounding him to stand their ground. And then, before spinning away from me, he caught my eyes again.

*Good-bye*, I said silently. *I love you.*

As if I'd spoken the words aloud, his eyes widened and he faltered.

Yes, I had to let him know that he hadn't loved me in vain. That I returned his love. I knew that now.

He stared at me, unable to sacrifice his love for me. His arms dropped. His swords began to slip out of his fingers.

"No-o-o-o!" I cried as Edgar's grip on my hair wrenched painfully. I couldn't let Collin give up. They'd kill him too. At least if he fought with the peasants, my uncle and cousin would only be able to kill me.

As one of Collin's swords clattered to the cobblestone street, I heard the distant trill of a trumpet outside the town gates. I ignored it and screamed my protest again. "No, Collin!"

How had I let Edgar get his hands on me in the first place? If only I'd been more cautious . . . But I'd been too focused on taking out the archers on the wall and keeping them from hurting Collin.

As it was, I'd already lost Bulldog. I wouldn't let Collin stand by and give up his life for me again.

"Kill me," I demanded of Sir Edgar. "Kill me this instant." At least if my cousin slit my throat now, Collin would have no reason to hand himself over to Uncle. Maybe he'd return to the fight before it was too late.

The trumpet blared again, this time louder. My attention was at last caught by the clatter of warhorses and the clank of armor, and my eyes flew to the town gate. At the sight of an army of knights, fully clad from head to toe in shining silver armor, brandishing an assortment of the most deadly weapons, dread swept into me and nearly knocked me off my feet.

How could we possibly fight against the rest of the Wessex army? Especially when they were mounted?

Behind me, Sir Edgar uttered an oath under his breath—an oath that expressed fear and dismay.

I took a closer look at the knights that charged down the cobbled street. At the front rode a tall knight with two imposing knights on either side. The single white cross painted on the shield of the tall knight in the center chased away my dread.

"The Noblest Knight," I whispered. The Duke of Rivenshire. The brother of the High King. And the two friends Collin had spoken of—Sir Derrick and Sir Bennet.

I'd dispatched a letter to the duke the same night I'd convinced Bulldog to help me with the revolt, but I hadn't expected that the duke would really come or that he'd have time to gather his most valiant warriors.

I wanted to release a cheer. But Edgar yanked me backward with him, his knife unrelenting against my throat. He must know that he couldn't defeat the duke and his army of ruthless, well-trained soldiers. They'd earned the reputation of being the best in the land.

Was Edgar planning to hold me hostage? Or would he kill me now anyway?

He dragged me farther back to the edge of the scaffolding, to the ladder.

Once again my gaze collided with Collin's. Whatever happened, I could rest assured that my uncle would be defeated. I'd survived the battle long enough to know that Collin would live. And that my people would finally have peace and security.

Collin shook his head, his eyes pleading with me not to give up yet. Then, before I knew what was happening, he sprinted toward the town wall. He dropped to a roll and out of sight.

The duke entered the market square with his sword drawn, his enormous horse snorting—evidence of the hard ride he'd made to arrive in Wessex. As he drew nearer, Edgar positioned me in front of his body.

I shuddered. He was planning to use me as a human shield. And there was no telling what else he'd do to me in order to ensure his safety.

An arrow ripped through the air. The hiss of it came close to my shoulder, but at Edgar's cry, I knew the sharp tip had pierced him instead, in the arm holding the knife to my throat.

A glance in the direction of the town wall told me that Collin had located the bow and arrows of a fallen archer. And now he was using the weapon to free me from Edgar.

I held myself absolutely still just as another arrow sliced past me and punctured Edgar's throat. He gave a gurgled cry as his eyes widened with surprise and then resignation. He started to sway, but before I could move, he fell against me and plunged his knife into my chest.

The tip sliced deep and a scream of agony ripped from my lips. I writhed at the burning fire that tore through me. But the weight of my cousin's body against mine pushed me backward. Suddenly, I felt myself fall over the side of the scaffolding, smashing into the ground with a thud that took away my breath. Then black oblivion hit me and delivered me from the pain.

# Chapter
## 20

*My eyelids fluttered open. A lacey white canopy the* color of angel's wings greeted me. I seemed to be floating in the softness of a cloud with warmth enveloping me.

Had I died and gone to heaven?

I squinted to see through the crack in gauzy bed curtains to the room beyond, to the tapestry on the wall. It was strangely familiar—the outline of a white pony in a field of red poppies.

Where was I?

With a start, I moved to sit up. But the motion caused my chest and right shoulder to burn in agony. I moaned and fell back.

A maid was immediately at my side, pressing a cool cloth against my forehead. A short man with gray hair fell into place next to the maid, and he was pouring a spoonful of foul-smelling liquid onto a spoon.

They both gave a start at the sight of me staring up at them.

The man smiled gently and the tension in his shoulders eased. "Lady Juliana, you're awake."

"Yes, 'twould appear that I am." I tried to regain my bearings, to make sense of where I was and all that had happened. All that I remembered was Edgar stabbing me and then falling off the scaffolding.

"Where am I and how long have I been unconscious?"

The maid brought a sliver goblet to my lips and lifted my head enough so that I could drink. Spiced ale filled my mouth and made a warm trail to my stomach.

"You've been sick for quite a few days, my lady," the man spoke kindly, touching the bandage upon my shoulder and the wound below. "We weren't sure you were going to survive, and so you're making us all very happy right now to see you're awake."

I decided he was likely the physician who had tended my stab wound. "I thank you for saving my life. I owe you much."

"No, my lady," the man said while shaking his head emphatically. "I'm honored to tend you. We are the ones who owe you our gratitude."

The door of the chamber opened and heavy footsteps crossed the room. Before I could react to make sure I was presentable, the physician stepped aside and I found myself staring up into the kind face of the Duke of Rivenshire.

"My child," he said softly. His face was regal, his hair lined with silver, and his bearing king-like. Even so, he wore humbleness like a cloak and the gentleness in his gaze probed me like that of a father.

"Your Grace." I tried to push myself up so that I could bow to him as I knew I ought.

"Stay where you are, my lady," he said. "You've suffered a great deal, and I would have you recover fully so that you can take your rightful place as ruler over your land."

I closed my eyes for an instant as overwhelming relief swelled in my chest. Ruler over my land. Was it possible that we'd won the battle? I opened my eyes again and swallowed the lump lodged there. "What has become of Uncle and my cousin?"

The duke's eyes crinkled at the edges, and I didn't know if it was with sadness, anger, or both. "Edgar is dead and Lord Wessex is in prison awaiting his sentencing—that is, if he lives. His wounds have festered."

I nodded and sank back into the plush pillows that cushioned my body. It was finally over. My people could live in freedom again. At that thought, tears pressed at the backs of my eyes.

With a deep breath, I pushed aside the emotions. "I thank you for coming to my aid, Your Grace. You and your men came at just the right time."

"I only wish we could have come sooner and spared you so much agony."

Over the duke's shoulder, I glimpsed one of his knights, a handsome dark-haired man with equally dark eyes. Where was the other? And Collin?

"This is Sir Bennet, my lady," the duke said in answer to my unspoken question.

The knight bowed but kept a respectable distance.

"My other knight, Sir Derrick, has returned home with haste to his bride. And I have put the rest of my men to work building homes and finding lodging for all of the peasants Lord Wessex had displaced. I hope you don't mind."

Hope burst through me. "Oh, Your Grace. I'm eternally grateful. I cannot begin to express it."

He smiled. "It's the least that we can do to help you."

At the thought of my companions having homes—real wattle and daub homes with thatched roofs to keep them warm in the cold months to come—my throat constricted with the need to cry out my relief.

"I'm sure you'll do much more for them once you take stock of your possessions and land," he continued. "But for now, at least they will have shelter and food."

I glanced around the chamber again. Something about the room stirred buried memories. "Where am I, Your Grace?"

"Don't you recognize it?"

I studied the tapestry of the white pony again. Understanding began to dawn in the deep recesses of my mind. I took in the white canopy and bed curtains, familiar arched windows with a stained glass circle forming the top pane.

"You're home," he said tenderly.

Home? Was I really back in the chamber that had belonged to me when I'd been a little girl?

"I'm only sorry I was so far away those many years ago, and unavailable to help your father defend his land. He was a good man."

"I wish I'd learned to follow his example sooner."

"You're learning now. And that's what matters." A flurry of gruff whispers came from the direction of the door. "I think the word has spread that you've woken," the duke said with a widening smile. "And there are many who would like to see you."

He waved his hand toward the newcomers, motioning them into the room.

Slow, hesitant footsteps crossed toward the bed. The duke stepped a respectable distance away and I found myself gazing up into Thatch's face, his blond hair sticking on end like usual. The bruises on his face had begun to turn a lighter purple.

"Thatch," I said softly, my eyes filling with tears again at the image of Bulldog lying in a pool of blood in the marketplace. He'd sacrificed himself so that his son could have a better life. The boy gave me gaping smile. "It's good to see you awake, Juliana—I mean, your ladyship."

I waved away his proper address, but I couldn't make my voice work past the sorrow clogging my throat—sorrow that I'd lost such a good friend. "You had to worry us like you usually do," he said. His arms were still heavily bandaged, but he held himself with a new maturity.

"I'm sorry about Bulldog," I whispered, my voice thick. A tear trickled out, even though I worked to hold my grief back.

Thatch's brows shot up. "Oh, don't worry about him. He can take care of himself just fine."

At that, another body pushed past Thatch to stand at the edge of my bed. A gruff face appeared above mine. "Young missy, I ought to take a switch to your backside for all of your crazy stunts during that battle." Bulldog's voice was rough, but the gentleness in his eyes reached out to caress me.

"You're alive?" Tears blurred my vision and the lump in my throat pressed with achingly sweet relief. "I can't believe you survived." Only then did I notice the thick bulge in his tunic where he wore a bandage against the wound in his side.

"I'm too stubborn and mean to die." His eyes brimmed with tears.

My smile wavered with the need to weep in his arms. We'd been through much together. And I loved him like a father.

He reached a hand to my cheek and brushed at my loose tear. "Besides, someone's got to be here to boss you around and keep you out of danger."

I laughed shakily and then captured his hand into mine, squeezing his fingers and the nub of his thumb. "Thank you," I whispered.

He nodded, and his eyes shone with a mixture of pride and love. We'd done it together. We'd finally accomplished what my father had set out to do. And it had taken more courage and sacrifice than either of us had realized we'd need.

The door of the room then banged against the wall with a force that left the walls trembling. "I heard she's awake," came a loud voice.

*Collin?*

My heart quivered with both anticipation and nervousness at the thought of seeing him again. I licked my lips and combed my fingers through my loose curls.

Collin's hurried footsteps neared the bed. Bulldog stepped away and pulled Thatch with him. As he nodded at Collin, his expression filled with the utmost respect.

Collin ducked between the lacy bed curtains and underneath the canopy. "Juliana?" He was breathing heavily, as if he'd run quite a distance at top speed. His tunic was covered in dust and straw, his hair in disarray, and he had several days of scruff on his jaw. His green eyes were bright and filled with an ocean full of worry.

Even in disarray, he'd never looked better, and my heart pattered harder. "I see you've cleaned yourself up a tad since the last time I saw you."

At my light tone, he paused. Then he grinned and flicked a piece of straw from his arm. "Just a tad, although I was quite sorry to lose the dungeon stench, especially since I knew you liked it so much."

Happiness spread from my heart throughout my body like the warmth of heating stones.

"And you've recovered from your abuses?" I asked, noting the purple bruise around his neck where the noose had almost strangled him.

"I've a few bumps and bruises yet, but nothing that can't heal." His smile grew. I knew he was minimizing his aches and pains to keep me from worrying. "I'm only sorry I didn't arrive earlier to spare you the dragging through town."

"Yes, that would have been sweet of you," he said. "But I do have to thank you for the very nice job you did slicing the noose."

"You're quite welcome." I loved bantering with him. And I couldn't imagine going the rest of my life without these exchanges. But would *he* want to spend his life with me, after I'd rejected him once already and sent him away?

As if sensing the turn of my thoughts, he lowered himself to his knees beside my bed. "I don't know whether to throttle you or thank you for coming back and rescuing me."

"You saved my life. So I thought it only fair that I save yours."

"That was so considerate of you." He grinned. "And now that I've saved yours once more, I guess I'll need to go out and find another way for you to rescue me."

I gave a soft laugh but then winced at the pain the motion caused in my chest.

His smile faded, replaced by a seriousness I hadn't witnessed in him before. He reached out and grazed my cheek. The simple caress sent a jolt through my body, stopping my heartbeat and my breathing. "I've been wild with worry over you," he admitted with an agonized whisper. "I should have thought to shoot the knife out of Edgar's hand first."

I silenced him with a touch of my fingers to his lips. "It's not your fault. You did everything you possibly could. If not for you, I'd be dead for certain."

He grasped my hand, opened my palm, and then brought his lips against the sensitive skin there. The warmth of his kiss, the heat of his breath, and the urgency of his hold sent another sizzling bolt into my middle. "Oh, Juliana," he breathed.

I longed to comb the hair off his forehead and to pull him closer. But I knew neither were appropriate, especially since we had a roomful of onlookers.

As if remembering the same, he released my hand and moved back. "I've been doing everything I can day and night to help your people. We're building them homes, providing them supplies for winter, and even helping many of them locate jobs."

A lump rose again in my throat. "You're a good man, Collin Goodrich," I whispered. "And I regret the day I accused you of anything less."

He met my gaze then, probing deep into my heart as if attempting to read all that was written there. I hoped he could see the truth, that I was sorry I'd sent him away.

"If I'm a good man, it's only because of you," he said. "You've shown me what it means to be a kind leader, to truly look at the needs of my people, and to show them compassion."

"You've always had those qualities. You just needed someone to help bring them out of you."

The longing upon his face was palpable, but with the utmost restraint he pulled back and stood. "As soon as I'm done overseeing the building of the homes here on your land, I'll be returning home so that I can make sure my own poor tenants are well-equipped to weather the coming winter."

I wanted to tell him not to go, to stay with me forever. But I knew I couldn't do that any more than I could have asked him to stay in my forest home with me. He belonged on his land, being a good lord to his own people.

"Whatever can I do to repay you for your kindness to me?" I asked.

He was silent for a long moment. His face was shadowed and much too serious.

Having watched our entire exchange, Sir Bennet stepped to Collin's side and clamped him across the shoulders. He squeezed as if in sympathy for his friend before looking at me. "Lady Juliana, I believe there is only one way you can ever repay your kindness to my dear friend Lord Collin."

"Anything, sir. I will do anything for him."

Sir Bennet smiled, and the motion was so fluid and beautiful, it would have taken my breath away had I not had eyes only for Collin.

"Then you must put him out of his terrible misery."

"Terrible misery?" I asked, noting that Collin's head and shoulders had slumped with dejection. What had happened now to cause him such misery? "And how may I do that?"

"You must agree to marry him." Sir Bennet slapped Collin across the back.

Collin's head shot up and mortification thundered across his features. He punched his friend in the arm good-naturedly. "You know she doesn't want to. And that's all right. At least we can be friends and neighbors, can't we?"

He turned his gaze upon me.

My heart welled with love for this man, this kind, sweet, funny man. Bulldog had been right; if my father had been there, he would have approved whole-heartedly of Collin. The problem was, Collin was too noble to ask me to marry him again. Even if he'd glimpsed love in my eyes that day of the battle, when I'd said my silent good-bye, he was determined to spare me further embarrassment.

If I wanted to marry Collin, I would have to take the offer Sir Bennet had so kindly placed before me.

"Sir Bennet is right," I said nervously. "If you're in such terrible misery, then I must do my part to help you. I must most certainly save you from such extreme desolation."

After a quick intake of breath while his eyes searched mine, a grin tugged at his lips.

"Besides, I don't really want to be neighbors with you."

His left brow quirked. "Are you saying that if I tossed you over my shoulder and carried you back to my castle, you wouldn't run away this time?"

"I promise, I'll never run away again, except to be where you are."

His lips curved into a full smile that reached into his eyes and set them glimmering with all the glory of sunshine. "Then I promise to never go anywhere unless you're by my side."

I reached a hand to him. He captured it and bent to place the softest of kisses on the end of my fingertips.

"I love you." I whispered the words that reverberated through every corner of my heart.

"I thought you'd never say it."

"I can't wait to say it to you every day for the rest of my life."

He slipped again to his knees at the side of my bed. "I shall indeed be the happiest man alive to hear it."

My chest ached with the need to hear his declaration, to know with certainty that he'd forgiven me for rejecting him and to know that he loved me in return.

He reached into the pouch at his side, tugged at it, retrieved something from its depths, then held out his hand. "I once told you that I wanted you to have this." He opened his fingers. There in his palm was his thick silver ring emblazoned with the cross of diamonds.

"I don't deserve it," I whispered.

"I never stopped loving you," he said softly, seriously. "And I never will. I will always love you. No matter what."

His declaration poured over my soul, chasing away the anxiety and making me love him even more.

He slipped the ring onto my thumb, back where it belonged. "Even though I'm a nobleman, will you do me the honor of marrying me and becoming my wife?"

I pressed the ring against my heart. "You're the noblest man I've ever met. And because of that, I can do nothing less than give you my whole heart, soul, and body."

"Is that a yes?"

"Yes."

He rose and gave a whoop that filled the chamber and filled my heart with overwhelming joy.

# Chapter
## 21

*"Keep your eyes closed," Collin said, his tone laced* with eagerness.

I smiled and pressed my eyelids together tighter, even though his hand over my eyes was enough.

My robe swirled above my wedding gown, and the thick fur gloves warmed my fingers against the frosty morning air. The late autumn sunshine poured down upon my loose hair like a blessing from heaven. I had no doubt that blessing was from my father looking down upon me, happy for me on my wedding day. I was about to join my life to the best man in the whole kingdom, and I knew my father would be deeply grateful that someone like Collin Goodrich loved me and would take vows to cherish and keep me all the days of his life.

"Just a little farther," Collin said, his breath near my neck making me shiver with delight.

We'd had to wait several weeks for both of us to fully recover from our wounds, and now that we were fully healed, we'd planned the wedding to take place outdoors in the forest that spanned both of our lands. We'd invited all the peasants that I'd lived with for so many years.

To show his appreciation to my people for rising up and helping me fight Lord Wessex, Collin had planned a feast so lavish for them that his cooks and mine had been busy for days baking in preparation. And of course, he'd planned an archery contest for afterward, to prove once and for all which one of us was the better archer.

"Ready yet?" I asked with a smile, leaning back against the solidness of his chest and relishing his nearness, not nearly ready for the moment of closeness to end.

"Almost."

I could hear the grin in the word, even if I couldn't see it.

He finally stopped. He pressed a gentle kiss against my ear and then followed it with a whisper. "My lady, your wedding present."

With that, he dropped his hand away from my eyes.

I blinked against the bright sunshine and then my gaze came to rest upon a breathtaking sight. There in front of me stood a beautiful white palfrey. Its immaculately groomed coat and bright eyes shone in the morning light. It tossed its head and neighed to greet me.

My heart swelled with unspeakable delight and brought a tremble to my lips.

"So . . . what do you think?" Collin asked, studying me, his brows arched with anticipation. "It's not quite a pony, but it's close."

I could only reach for his hand and intertwine my fingers through his and squeeze. "Oh, Collin," I managed, my eyes flooding with sudden tears.

He was the sweetest man I'd ever met.

At his grin, I knew he understood just how deeply his gift had moved me.

Nearby, in a clearing in the woodlands, stood my companions. Some sat on rocks, others on logs. A few of the children had even climbed into the trees to watch the wedding. Their faces were wreathed in smiles.

The Duke of Rivenshire stood in the center of the clearing, smiling at us. Beside him were Collin's two closest friends, Sir Bennet and Sir Derrick.

Closest to the palfrey stood Bulldog and Thatch. They were adorned in new tunics, cloaks, and finely tailored leather boots. Their faces were scrubbed clean and they wore fashionable felt hats. They too grinned at me, their eyes shining with pride.

At Collin's suggestion, I'd put Bulldog in charge of my estate. He and Thatch would live in and manage my castle, using it as a refuge for anyone in need. I'd appointed Bulldog to make sure that no one on my land would ever again be in want.

Of course I would still visit my holdings and help in the ruling. But I'd been gone from my estate for so long, and after the pain I'd suffered there, I was all too content to live with Collin in Goodrich Castle. I was ready to start over, to make a new life for myself, to rule with benevolence and kindness next to Collin.

Lady Irene had insisted that Collin send her to live in a convent, at least until she could recover from the terrors of all that had happened. Fortunately, Mistress Higgins and William had been rescued with minimal damage. Apparently, Thatch's torture had given my uncle all the information he'd needed, so except for being sorely frightened and slightly starved, Collin's loyal servants had survived unscathed.

"I have one more wedding gift for you," Collin said, drawing me into the crook of his arm. "At least one more gift for now. I'll have plenty more later."

I laughed softly. "You know I don't want anything. I have everything I need in you."

His arms tightened around me. "But I adore spoiling you."

"You adore spoiling everyone." I'd learned his generosity to those in need knew no bounds.

"Well, I especially enjoy spoiling you." He motioned at two young peasant girls who approached me carrying baskets. They were adorned in pretty pink gowns, likely the finest they'd ever seen or owned. I had no doubt Collin had ordered them made for the girls especially for the wedding.

They came before me with shy smiles and curtsied at my feet. Then they each held their baskets toward me. "For you, my lady."

I bestowed smiles upon them and took one of the baskets. I tugged off the silver-threaded linen, and there inside were dozens upon dozens of strawberries, fully ripe and beautifully red.

I gasped. "Where did you find these at this time of year?"

"I had to search far and wide." He picked up a plump berry and held it up. "But it was worth it, because they're my favorite fruit."

"And your atonement for your long-ago insult?" I teased.

"Yes, my way of begging you to finally forgive me, sweetheart," he replied playfully. "Don't you know that whenever a young boy teases a girl, it's only because he likes her?"

"You must have *really* liked me."

"I still *really* like you." His voice dipped low and did funny things to my stomach. "And I love your hair."

"I forgive you," I said rather breathlessly. "As long as you promise to give me a basket of strawberries every year in payment."

Gently, he turned me so that we were facing each other. He combed his fingers into the long curls of my strawberry-red hair that the wind teased about my shoulders. "Promise." The one word held so many possibilities, and promises of laughter, friendship, and days of ruling our people wisely together.

He brought a fistful of my curls to his lips and kissed them. His eyes also promised many more kisses, and my knees grew weak at the thought. "I have searched far and wide," he whispered, "and have finally found the one my heart desires."

His love for me made me speechless. "You've taught me what it means to sacrifice of myself," he continued, "and I plan to spend the rest of my life sacrificing for you again and again."

I could do nothing less for him. "Since you would like to sacrifice yourself for me," I said, glancing toward all of our loyal friends who were still watching us. "Then why don't you start right now."

"Anything, my lady," he said so earnestly, I couldn't contain my smile.

"I know how hard it will be to give me a kiss," I said teasing him again. "But perhaps you can make the sacrifice and give me just a small one?"

A light sparkled in his eyes. "It will be a very hard sacrifice to make. But since I've pledged to do anything, then I shall force myself to meet your request."

"You're so kind, my lord," I whispered as he bent nearer, his gaze fixed upon my lips. "You are indeed sacrificial—"

His lips cut off my words and met mine with the sweetness and promise of a lifetime of love . . . and sacrifice.

# Epilogue

*I perched on the high branch of the sycamore and* held myself absolutely still. The twine of my bow touched my cheekbone. My sights were trained upon my target in the distance through the fresh green of June foliage.

I tried to ignore a crack on the branch behind me and the warm breath that suddenly bathed the back of my neck. A soft brush of a kiss sent heat pulsing through my veins. The strong but gentle fingers of the man I loved splayed around my waist, burning through the linen of my bodice.

"Mmmm . . ." he whispered against my ear. "You taste like fresh-plucked strawberries."

I knew what he was attempting to do. And it wouldn't work today. "You're not distracting me," I said.

"We'll see about that." His lips moved to the tender spot between my neck and shoulder blade. The warmth of his kiss made me suck in a breath.

I squinted harder at the target, pressed my full weight into the horn, pulled back the string, and then let the arrow loose. At that very same moment, Collin's mouth found the pulsing vein beneath my ear. As he laid claim to it, my hand slipped just slightly. It was enough so that when, a moment later, my arrow hit the target, I missed the center by at least a finger's length.

"I won," he said, pulling back and peering at the target in triumph, a wicked grin alighting his face. "I'm the most irresistible."

I leaned back into him and let him nuzzle my neck to his heart's content. I couldn't argue with him. He was completely irresistible. Every time he kissed me, I melted like tallow.

"You know as well as I do that the only way you can win our archery contests is by distracting me." I shifted on the branch so that I was more securely within his strong embrace, facing him, letting him kiss my nose, my cheeks, and finally my lips.

For a long moment the world around us disappeared. I forgot about the servants awaiting us at the base of the tree, the judge standing near the target, and the new page boy who'd been assigned to retrieve our arrows.

Even though we'd been married since last fall and we'd spent all winter together, I never tired of Collin's kisses or the way he held me. And he never tired of kissing me every opportunity he could.

"You might be the most irresistible," I said breathlessly when he finally pulled back. "But I'm still the best archer."

"But my arrow hit the target in spite of your efforts to divert me," he said with a grin. "So I think that makes me the most irresistible and the best archer both."

Yes, in spite of my distractions while he'd taken his shot, he'd hit the center exactly. Although he'd shivered in delight at the tempting kisses I'd planted on his ear and jaw and neck, he hadn't budged from his exactness.

Even so, when I had both of my feet planted solidly on the ground without his nearness to distract me, I was quicker and more accurate than him every time.

I combed my fingers through his silky, windswept hair. "The only way you can beat me is by cheating."

The bright green of his eyes matched the new growth that had turned the Goodrich lands into a lush wilderness. Although we lived in his castle, there were still many days when I couldn't resist the call to be back in the woods, amidst the place that had been home to me.

"Admit it," I teased. "You have to distract me in order to win. It's your only line of defense."

His grin inched higher. "And just what will the fair lady give me if I admit it?"

A call in the woods behind us interrupted our tryst. The tone was urgent and I could feel Collin's muscles tense at the same time as mine. Although we'd had peace in our combined lands since my uncle's rule had finally come to an end, I was under no illusion that we'd be problem free forever.

"I've a missive for Lord Goodrich," came the voice again, sharp and commanding.

Collin jumped from the branch and landed upright in the leaves below. He reached up and assisted me down. Although I didn't need his help, I relished it anyway.

When we were both on the ground, we faced an armed rider on a large warhorse. At the sight of his coat of arms, a white cross within a backdrop of silver, my heart gave a leap of recognition. The knight was riding on behalf of the Noblest Knight, the Duke of Rivenshire.

I expected Collin to flash a grin and his features to light up at the sight of his mentor's messenger. But instead the muscles in his face turned to granite. "What news do you bring me?"

The knight didn't dismount. Instead, he thrust a rolled parchment into Collin's hands as though in a hurry to be on his way. "The duke requests your assistance, my lord."

Collin rapidly broke the wax seal on the letter, opened it, and began to read. When he was finished, his expression was grave. "How long has the siege been in effect?"

"At least four weeks," the messenger replied. "And we've gotten word that the residents are near starvation."

Collin straightened to his full, imposing height, the muscles in his arms rippling. He folded the letter and nodded to the knight. "You may tell your master that I shall join him just as quickly as I'm able to saddle my horse."

The knight nodded curtly then spurred his steed away, disappearing the way he'd come almost as if he'd never arrived. However, Collin's changed mood told me that the situation was real and dangerous. And when his green eyes met mine, I knew I would lose him—at least for a short time.

"The duke has called for my help," he explained, although I'd already surmised as much.

I nodded at him to continue.

"My fellow knight, Sir Bennet, is in terrible danger," Collin said. "He and his family are under attack from a neighboring lord. They're being held under siege within the walls of their castle with no way of escape."

I knew of whom he spoke—the dark-haired and handsome young knight who had come to help us during our time of need. He'd been one of Collin's best friends and closest companions while he grew up in and fought for the household of the Duke of Rivenshire.

"The situation is grave," Collin said, his expression severe as though he were already anticipating the battle that was to come. "And the duke is calling me to ride with him to help save Bennet's life."

"Is it even possible?" I asked, knowing full well that if Sir Bennet's castle had been under siege for some time, the fortress may have been weakened and possibly breached. Even as we spoke, Sir Bennet and his family could already have been taken prisoner or put to death.

The fear in Collin's eyes told me that he'd come to the same conclusion. "I don't know if we'll be able to save Bennet.

But I have to join forces with the duke and ride to Windsor land to Maidstone Castle in Hampton, and we have to try."

I nodded my understanding. He had to go. There was no other choice. And even though I couldn't bear the thought of being parted from Collin and even though I was tempted to beg him to take me along, my presence would only bring him further worry. He'd be able to fight the battle more whole-heartedly and valiantly if he didn't have to think about protecting me.

"I'll miss you," I said, watching him tighten the leather arrow pouch at his side. He'd already called for the servants to bring him his horse. For a moment he was distracted, and I knew he'd already switched into warrior mentality and was already preparing himself for the battle that was to come.

He took the reins of his horse and readied himself to swing up into his saddle. I had the sudden desire to fling myself at him and plead with him to stay, to continue our lover's games, to never leave me. Now that I'd had Collin and marriage and had experienced love, I didn't want to lose it.

But at the same time, I realized he could do nothing less than what he'd been born to do: be a champion and fight for those in need, even if it meant he might sacrifice his life in the process.

As though sensing the danger of what was to come, and sensing that he might not see me again, he dropped his reins and crossed to me in two swift strides. His arms closed about me, and he dragged me against him in a crushing hug that was followed by his lips claiming mine. His kiss seared me deeply. Each move of his lips against mine told me of how precious I was to him, how much he loved me, and that I would be his through eternity.

When he finally broke our kiss, we were both breathless. I had to work hard to hold back my tears. For in my heart,

I realized the kiss was also his good-bye, and that it could possibly be the last time I ever tasted of our love.

With one last, piercing look, he released me, leaving me cold and shivering in spite of the warm early summer sunshine. As I watched him mount, I prayed fervently that the kiss would not be the last, and that we would still have many more in the days and years to come. And I prayed that he would not only be able to return to me, but be able to do so swiftly.

"You take my heart with you," I whispered in a choked voice as he spurred his horse away. "Godspeed."

# Discussion Questions

1. What are some of the characteristics that drew Juliana and Collin to each other? What are some of the qualities that they had in common? What made them a good fit for each other?

2. While physical attractions can be strong, why do you think it's important to be drawn to someone for more than their outward appearance?

3. Juliana and Collin spent time getting to know each other by immersing themselves in each other's world. Why do you think it's important for couples to spend time really getting to see the other person in their daily life (rather than always prettied-up on dates)?

4. Juliana was honest with Collin about his shortcomings. She challenged him to become a better and more caring ruler. How can couples be honest with one another without being hurtful?

5. Juliana and Collin first kiss was on the tower after she opened up about her past suffering. Why do you think we crave intimacy when we're hurting? Why is it even more important during those painful times to be careful about putting ourselves in risky situations?

6. When Juliana sees Collin's bare chest in the cave, the sight affects her. Usually, we think visual stimulation only affects men—but visual images can also stir up lust in women. Why is modesty so important for both men and women? And what does modesty mean for you?

7. Feeling physical reactions to the opposite sex is completely normal. However, it's what we do with those reactions that counts. Why is it important to set boundaries ahead of a situation, rather than waiting until you're faced with the temptation?

8. Juliana and Collin had chaperones most of the time, due to the historical time period. Should couples today ever be alone? When can being alone become dangerous?

9. Collin literally gave up everything in order to save Juliana from burning at the stake. In what ways did his sacrifice for Juliana resemble Christ's sacrifice for us? Would you have made the same decisions?

10. In the end, Juliana, too, realizes that she can sacrifice for the greater good of her people, and for Collin. How important is sacrifice in a relationship? What does the Bible say about relational sacrifices? How does that contradict the current me-first philosophy of the world?

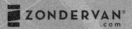